OPERATION SUNSET

SUSAN HAYES

ABOUT THE BOOK

She's the woman he can't forget... and the one he can never have.

Three years ago, Crispen met the woman of his dreams, only to discover they were about to be co-workers, too. Aria had rules against mixing business and pleasure, so he'd taken the next best option and become her best friend... until he had to make a decision that changed the course of both their lives.

Now, what's left of their friendship will be tested. They're going undercover to take down one of Nova Force's greatest enemies, and they'll have no one to rely on but each other.

She thought she couldn't have it all. Had she been wrong?

Aria lost more than her leg in the explosion that nearly ended her career. She's still counting the costs, but she's afraid that at the top of the list is the

only man who got past her walls and into her heart
—Crispen.

Their new assignment puts them in enemy territory with dubious intel, no backup, and a plan that didn't survive first contact with reality. To finish their mission, they'll have to risk more than their lives... they'll have to put their hearts in the line of fire.

1

Cris left the *Malora's* med-bay the moment the computer announced he was cleared to return to duty. While he still believed that doctors made the worst patients, after a single day of bedrest he was willing to admit that medics were almost as bad.

Or maybe it was just him.

His face was still a little tender in spots and his skin itched in some unpleasant places, but Dr. Li had assured him it would only be a matter of hours before his new medi-bots repaired the last traces of the surgical alterations.

"Don't poke at it and it will heal faster, Lieutenant," had been Tyra's parting advice when she'd left the med-bay a few hours ago. She'd said it was to let him rest, but he was pretty sure she just needed to get away from his grumpy ass. He'd have to apologize and claim it was pre-mission jitters.

She might even pretend to believe it.

His team was a tightknit crew that had grown even closer since circumstances had forced them to live on board the *Malora*. Astek Station was being decommissioned after the Grays' last attack, and their new home was still under construction. For security reasons, Dante's family was on board too. Nico was a key witness in an upcoming trial against Bellex Corp and Tyra was openly affiliated with both Nova Force and the group of rebellious cyborgs currently sitting at the top of the Gray Men's hit list.

It made for a crowded ship with limited personal space and even less privacy. As the only single team member on board, he knew far more than he wanted to about the sex lives and relationship challenges of his teammates. It also meant they knew why he was on edge these days, and it had almost nothing to do with his surgical alterations or even the fact this might be his last mission with this team.

It was because he'd be seeing *her* again.

They were on their way to collect the missing member of their crew. Aria had made a full recovery and was ready to reclaim her place on the team, which was wonderful news. The problem was, he didn't know if her return meant it was time for him to leave. Team Three had been her crew before it had been his. If she couldn't forgive him for his failures, he should be the one to go. He'd taken enough from her already. He wouldn't take her family, too.

An excited whoop pierced the air, snapping him out of his broody thoughts.

"I'm going to beat you again! You're too slow, Mama."

Two seconds later, a small pair of feet appeared at the top of a nearby ladder and Nico leaped down, trusting the grav-plate to catch him before he landed on the deck.

"One day, one of those is going to fail and you're going to break both your ankles," Cris said.

"That's what Mama says, too, but it hasn't happened yet!" Nico replied and then turned to look at Cris. The boy's grin vanished and his entire demeanor changed. He dropped into a fighter's crouch and raised his fists, looking like a miniature replica of his adopted father.

"Who the *fraxx* are you?"

Veth. He'd forgotten about the changes to his appearance. "Easy, Booster Rocket. It's just me, Caldwell."

The boy's eyes narrowed. "Lieutenant?"

"Yup. Your mama did a good job making me look different. Didn't she?"

Nico's hands dropped and his eyes widened in surprise. "Holy *fraxx*, it is you!"

The soft hiss of the mag-lift doors opening filled the momentary silence.

"Language, Nico!" Tyra scolded as she stepped into the corridor.

"Busted," Cris murmured in sympathy.

Nico's face fell. "Sorry, Mama. But the lieutenant surprised me!"

Cris waved at his face. "The first real-world test of my new disguise was a success."

"Ah. In that case, I suppose we can make an exception." Tyra wagged a finger at Nico. "But only this one time. We're going to be arriving at the colony soon and I expect you to be on your best behavior for at least the first three days."

"Three days?" Nico wailed. "Dad said two."

Tyra raised a dark brow and Nico hung his head in defeat. "Three days. I can do that."

"I know you can." She pulled the boy into a hug that lasted until he squirmed in protest.

"I'm going to be late for my robotics lesson with Magi—I mean Ensign Erben. I need to go, Mama."

"Go on. Have fun and try not to blow up anything."

Nico rolled his eyes. "That happened one time." He waved at them and then took off down the corridor at a speed that would have made some athletes jealous.

Tyra watched him go with a wry smile. "I'm still not convinced giving him the medi-bot treatment was a good idea. He had too much energy *before* we dosed him with nanotech."

"But now at least you and Dante can keep up

with him." Everyone on the team had taken the treatment, and the offer had been extended to immediate family members. Tyra and Nico were the only ones who hadn't had nanotech already, and within hours of their reunion with Dante, he'd taken them for their injections. It had nearly killed the big man, not knowing if they were safe after Astek Station was attacked.

Cris had gotten a taste of that feeling as well when their last mission had gone sideways. None of them had expected the Gray Men to sacrifice six of their own in an explosion meant to take out his team. When Nyx and Aria were caught in the blast, he'd experienced the worst pain of his life while waiting to see if they made it out. Then he'd gone through something even more painful when Nyx had appeared with Aria's battered, mangled body in her arms.

Months later, the memory of that day was still enough to make his heart ache. To save her life, he'd had to carve off pieces of his best friend, the woman he'd wanted for years. No one could expect forgiveness for something like that. He'd taken her leg and left her with two choices—leave the job she loved or accept the nanobot treatment and a cybernetic limb to replace the one she'd lost.

She hadn't quit the team.

"Do you think she's going to like the new look?" Tyra asked softly.

He didn't need to ask who Tyra meant. He gave what he hoped was an indifferent shrug. "I doubt she'll notice."

"Going against the odds? That's not like you."

"What odds?" he asked, but he already had a good idea who to blame.

Tyra laughed. "No one told you? The current odds are seven-to-one she does a double take the first time she sees you."

"I'm going to kill Magi."

Tyra's lips twitched as she tried to stifle more laughter. "It wasn't his idea. You'll have to take that up with Nyx. Apparently she got the numbers from Chance, though."

"Chance. The cyborg who can calculate odds with almost omnipotent accuracy? Why is she involved in..." He groaned and started to bury his face in his hands. Then he remembered he wasn't supposed to touch that area yet. "The Nova Club crew are taking bets on this?"

She patted his arm. "I'm afraid so. I made my bet before I started your surgery. Now I've seen the result, I think I should have doubled the amount. She isn't going to recognize you."

"You think surgery changed me that much?" He'd been surprised at the difference in his appearance, but he still saw himself beneath the changes. His cheekbones were higher now, his nose given an artificial bump to make it look as if it had been broken a few times, and his eyes, hair and skin color had been altered. A few other minor cosmetic tweaks and he'd been changed enough that no facial recognition software would be able to connect his new identity to one Lieutenant Crispin Caldwell, known officer of Nova Force.

"The procedures are part of it, but that's not all that's changed." Tyra raised one dark brow and gave him an assessing look. "You've spent hours in the gym since you got back. I've seen your charts. I know how much muscle mass you've put on lately. It's changed the way you look and move. You're different now, Trip."

"Yeah?" He gave her an exaggerated grin and flexed his biceps, puffing out his chest at the same time. "Do you think I'm ready to take on Buttercup?"

She laughed and shook her head. "Not yet. Dante has genetics on his side. But I wouldn't bet against you if you went up against Sabre."

"I'm not going to test that theory, but I appreciate the thought." He had no intention of testing his skills against the team's second in command. That was a no-win scenario. Either he got his ass handed to him or he wound up on kitchen cleanup duty for a month.

"Probably a wise choice. He's been grumpy since Bobbi left to start up the new legal team."

"And once we drop you and Booster off at Haven, Dante's going to be in a foul mood, too. We better be fully stocked up on ice cream and chocolate or morale is going to crash and crater."

Tyra smiled, but the expression didn't reach her eyes. "You'll take care of him for me?"

"Of course. That's one of the few parts of my job I'm still needed for. But honestly, the best thing for Dante will be knowing you two are safe and well-protected. The colony is about the safest place I can think of. After that last attempt to mess with their nanotech, the entire population is on high alert." He winked at her. "And besides, you are going as guests of royalty, with a suite of rooms in the palace and everything. Nico might never want to leave."

"That's going to take some getting used to. I don't suppose you have any pointers for me? I heard your family rules a planet."

Years of practice made it easy to hide his reaction, but he still felt it. The twist in his gut as his past came out of the shadows to sink its claws into the life he'd built after leaving home.

"It's only half a planet," he corrected her with a light, bantering tone and a genial smile. "Just be yourself. From what I understand, the prince and his *anrik* aren't much for courtly protocols and their mate is a human cyber-jockey with authority issues. You'll be fine."

Tyra smiled. "That's what your sister said, too."

"She's pretty smart. Not as smart or as charming as me, of course, but she's a close second." He gestured to his face. "I'll have to message her soon and show her your handiwork."

"She won't recognize you at first."

He grinned. "Then maybe I should make sure her three husbands are home when I message. A little jealousy is good for a relationship... or so I've heard."

Tyra shot him a wicked little smile and then launched an unexpected verbal salvo. "I've discovered that the most important thing in any relationship is honesty. You should probably try that sometime."

She left him reeling from the impact of her words and headed off down the hall toward the med-bay.

They all thought this was something that could be fixed with a few simple words. That if he just told Aria how he felt, things would all fall into place for the two of them.

They were wrong.

Aria knew exactly how he felt about her. Their chemistry had been hotter than a super nova from the moment they met. That hadn't stopped her from ending things the moment he'd walked into his first team meeting and discovered they weren't just lovers... they were teammates.

Soon, they might not even be that.

Honesty wasn't going to fix this. He didn't know what could. If this was their last mission together, he'd do all he could to keep her safe. He'd failed her too many times already.

Shadow stepped into the gap beside Aria and gave her shoulder a squeeze. "Your leg might be cybernetic, but your lungs aren't. Try to remember to breathe," she commented.

"I'm fine. It's just strange seeing this from the other side." Aria turned to smile at her friend and then pointed upward. The *Malora* had broken through the cloud cover and was on final descent to the colony's largest landing zone. "Normally I'm on board and strapped in for this part."

"Mhhm." Shadow's noncommittal noise was accompanied by a knowing look.

"Having an empath for a friend is a *fraxxing* pain in the ass sometimes," Aria muttered.

"Try having one as a mate," Kade said with a wry chuckle. He and Denz were behind her, offering their quiet support. She appreciated it more than she could say.

She'd come to Haven for her rehabilitation because it was home to so many cyborgs, including one she knew —Shadow—her teammate Nyx's clone. Nyx had encouraged her to go, too, since she had needed somewhere to recover. Once she arrived, she'd quickly discovered that the cyborgs here were more than just a source of information and advice on adjusting to her new limb. As battle-scarred veterans, they understood her struggles and offered her support without judgment. The colony was like a second home now, and leaving it, and the friends she'd made, was harder than she'd expected. That's why she was feeling so emotional right now. It had nothing to do with seeing *him* again.

Nothing at all.

They watched in silence as the big ship landed, thrusters melting holes in the snow on the tarmac.

Only when the engines had shut down did Shadow speak again. "Are you anxious because you want to see him or because you don't?"

Aria shot her friend an irritated look. "Nyx told you? When?"

"Nyx told me what was going on before you even arrived here, but I had some of it figured out already." She tapped her temple. "Empath, remember?"

"You have no idea how grateful I am that's not a talent you share with Nyx, though I still don't understand how that's possible given you were cloned from her DNA."

"They tinkered." Shadow shrugged. "I try not to think about it too much."

"And you're avoiding the question," Deniz commented drolly.

Aria flipped him an obscene gesture over one shoulder without looking back. "If the three of you ever need a career change, Nova Force could use more skilled interrogators."

"That's not an answer either," Shadow said.

Aria huffed out an annoyed breath. "Yeah, yeah. The problem is I don't know the answer to that question."

Shadow took her hand and squeezed it lightly. "You'll figure it out. You're ready to go back."

"Damn right I am. I was born ready." Aria squared her shoulders as the main door opened and a ramp extended to the ground. "The question is... are they?"

Commander Dax Rossi was the first to appear, dressed in their standard blue and silver uniform. He scanned the small crowd and then smiled when he spotted Aria. His lips moved as he said something to the rest of the crew, and several more faces appeared in the doorway. She recognized them all. Trinity, Nyx, and even Nico raised a hand in greeting as they playfully jostled each other to be the next one down the ramp. Nico won.

"Behave!" Dante boomed as he stepped into view. Nico didn't pay any attention. The boy raced to the nearest drift of snow, whooped with joy and started making snowballs. The moment Dante set foot on the ramp, Nico started hurling snowballs at him, peppering the hull of the *Malora* but missing his father with all of them.

When he ran out of ammunition, the boy turned

and bolted, laughing and yelling, "Ah! Magi, help!"

"You're on your own, Booster! I warned you not to do it the minute we landed!" Eric called out as he descended, grinning. Nyx was already jogging toward them, her smile identical to the one her clone wore as Shadow ran out to meet her.

The only teammate she hadn't seen yet was Cris. She used her cybernetic eye to zoom in on the doorway. Was he staying on board? How would she feel if he did?

Before she could figure out the answer to that, someone else appeared at the door. It was a man she didn't know. He had platinum blond hair styled into tousled spikes, broad shoulders and a muscular build that spoke of hours of training time. His skin was a golden-brown shade that contrasted with his hair and made his aqua-blue eyes pop. Whoever he was, he was hotter than a supernova.

Then the stranger ran a hand through his hair in a gesture that was as familiar to her as the sound of her own voice.

Holy *fraxx*. Feelings she had refused to acknowledge for months welled up inside her. Was that... "Trip?" She didn't mean to say that last bit out loud and was grateful Shadow wasn't close enough to hear her.

At least she thought she wasn't, but a second later her friend's laughter-filled voice filled her head. "And now you know the answer to my question."

Aria didn't bother to reply on the internal comm channel she'd had implanted during her stay, instead speaking aloud. "Cyborg super-hearing is a pain in the ass!"

Behind her, Kade and Denz laughed.

At least the distraction saved her from staring at Cris like a slack-jawed fool. By the time she looked at him again, he was on the ground with the others. Now, they were making their way toward the group with Dax leading and Cris hanging toward the back.

Lieutenant Crispin Charles Caldwell the Fifteenth, though no one called him that. He was Triple C, or more often just Trip. It had to be him, but why did he look so different?

As Dax approached, she drew herself to attention, and the uniform that had felt too tight and itchy since putting it on suddenly felt familiar again. She saluted her commander and tried to ignore his broad smile as he saluted her in return. "Lieutenant Jessop, are you ready to return to duty?"

"Yes, sir."

"Excellent." His shoulders relaxed and his smile widened. "Then I believe you are about to be mobbed by the rest of this motley crew. It's good to see you again, Blink."

"Good to see you, too, Fido," was all she managed before she was caught up in a series of hugs and greetings from the rest of her team. She hadn't let herself acknowledge how much she'd missed them until now.

Only when he spoke did she realize Cris had come up behind her and set a hand on her shoulder.

"You look good, Jessop. Any trouble adjusting to..." he trailed off as she turned to look at him, her smile freezing into place as his words struck home. He'd been the first one to mention her new cybernetic limb. It might be because he was a medic, but when she looked up at him, he wasn't looking at her. His gaze was held by something just over her left shoulder.

He couldn't even look at her. She swallowed hard and clapped him on the shoulder. "I'm fine, Trip. Couldn't be better. You look good, too. You made some changes while I was gone. I bet the ladies love the new look."

"I..." he finally dropped his gaze to meet hers. "It's for a mission. Tyra only did it a few days ago. You think it will work?"

"You're going undercover?" She was too surprised to hide her shock. He didn't do undercover missions. He was too recognizable. Though that wouldn't be a problem this time. She hadn't recognized him and they'd worked together for years.

Dax joined the conversation, the crackle of command back in his voice. "He is. And if you're ready, Blink, so are you."

She was ready for any mission... but was she

ready to go undercover with someone who couldn't even look at her?

The answer came before she could dwell on it. "Yes, sir." It was the unspoken motto of Team Three. The mission always came first.

2

———

CRIS DIDN'T SLEEP. He tried, but every time he closed his eyes, he wound up revisiting his reunion with Aria again. Not his finest moment. All the polish and charm his politician father had drilled into him vanished the moment he'd opened his mouth.

That wasn't the worst part, though. It had been the look on her face when Dax had told her they'd be partners on this next mission. It wasn't anything obvious. Aria was too good at her job to give away much, but he knew her well enough to see the signs. She hadn't been happy about it, and that might be a serious problem. Undercover work was tricky, and if she didn't feel like she could trust him, it would affect the op.

He snorted at his attempt at self-delusion. He wasn't worried about the mission. He was worried about how to fix his relationship with Aria. He hadn't had any time to talk to her yesterday. She'd needed some time to get settled into her quarters on board the ship. Then they all headed out for dinner as guests of Phaedra and her mates.

Dinner had led to an invitation to visit a tavern, and the rest of the night had passed in a blur of laughter, drinks, and a great many beings who wanted to say goodbye to Aria—most of them male.

The more hugs and kisses she got, the deeper he'd disappeared into the shadows. He didn't want her memories of her farewell party tainted by the unresolved issues between them. He stayed out of her way while trying to make it look like that wasn't what he was doing.

It worked, mostly. She looked happy and relaxed... unless she looked at him.

But that had been yesterday. Today was a new day, and there was no point staying frustrated. Technological wonders were invented every day, but so far no one had figured out time travel. Until they did, he'd just have to move on.

Shoving his feelings aside, he donned a fresh uniform and went to grab breakfast in the galley. Most of the crew was off duty today, which meant the galley was abnormally quiet. He ate with nothing and no one to distract him from his thoughts.

He had half-hoped Aria would appear, but he knew the odds were against it. Even without the current tension between them, Aria wasn't much of a morning person. She was more of the "give me the coffee and don't make me talk until it's gone" type. She'd be in her quarters, caffeinating in solitude the way she always did.

He wouldn't see her until the briefing, which meant they wouldn't have time to talk first. *Veth.*

The briefing room door was closed and sealed with a "Do Not Disturb" icon flashing on the keypad when he arrived. He was early, so he leaned against the bulkhead across from the door to wait. Dax would open the door when he was ready to brief them.

Footsteps on the metal deck warned him someone else was coming down the corridor. He knew the cadence of those steps, the light footfalls that shouldn't have been possible for someone wearing combat boots.

Aria.

He stayed where he was, forcing himself to relax as she came into view. The way the light fell left him in a small patch of shadow, which meant she didn't see him right away. Her eyes were on the door to the briefing room, and she walked with the predatory grace he loved to watch. It had drawn him to her the first night they'd met, and he'd never get tired of seeing her prowl her way through life.

She'd been dancing in a dive bar that night. He'd only been on Ibix Station Seven for a few hours and was looking for a place to drink and collect his thoughts before he met the team the next day. The last thing in the galaxy he'd expected to find that night was the woman of his dreams.

She'd worn a black bodysuit with stripes of neon that glowed and flickered in the dim light of the dance floor. It had fit her like a second skin, adding to the effect of a hunter out looking for a meal.

He'd decided to volunteer to be dessert.

That had been three years, eight months, and seventeen days ago.

He'd never forgotten a detail of that evening. He tried to buy her a drink, but she'd refused and then surprised him by turning around not two seconds later and buying him one instead. Drinks had led to dancing. Dancing had led to talking and laughter, and laughter had led to the most incredible night of mind-blowing sex he'd ever had. Like everything else about Aria Jessop, it had been unforgettable. It had also been a onetime thing.

That was the past, though. And as he watched her move toward him, he wondered if he'd ever be able to recapture the magic they'd shared that night. The odds were not in his favor. They hadn't been for years. Not since he'd reported to his new assignment the next morning and found himself seated across the table from Lieutenant Aria Jessop, lead interrogator for Nova Team Three.

She'd called it off an hour later, telling him she

would never mix work with her social life and that the most she could offer him was her friendship. Now, he wasn't sure they even had that anymore.

His doubts amplified when she finally spotted him and immediately went stiff. Her easy grace vanished, her shoulders locked and jaw tense. She reached the doorway without saying a word, though she did nod in greeting.

He opened his mouth to say good morning but said something entirely different. "If you'd rather not do this mission with me, I can ask the commander to replace me."

Aria rolled her dark eyes. "Don't be stupid. You're here, I'm here, and we *can* do this. We're professionals. Besides, you've already been through the surgery. It would be a shame to waste all of Dr. Li's hard work trying to make you pretty."

Her insults put him a little more at ease. If she was willing to banter, even if it was just to make fun of his looks, maybe things weren't unfixable after all. He checked the corridor. No one else was around. Now might be a good time to...

Before he could apologize to her for what he'd had to do, the keypad switched from red to green and the door to the briefing room slid open.

"Enter," Dax called before either of them could announce themselves.

Cris pushed off the wall and gestured for Aria to go in first. As he moved in behind her, she looked back and gave him an appraising glance. "Is the physique yours or a temporary surgical illusion?"

"That's me." He gave a casual, one-shouldered shrug. "This team isn't going to need a medic much, so I figured it was time I diversified my skill set."

Dax made a noise somewhere between amusement and frustration. "Is that what you're calling your new training schedule? The rest of us have another word for it."

He rose from his seat at the table and rapped his knuckles on the dented surface. "Good to see you both. Take a seat."

Aria moved to the far side of the table from Cris and claimed a seat opposite him. "Training schedule?"

Dax nodded. "Didn't he tell you yet? He got certified as a sharpshooter, logged enough real and sim flight hours to get himself qualified as a pilot, and spent the rest of his time learning hand-to-hand combat techniques."

Aria's brows rose at the same time her draw dropped. "No, he didn't tell me. I leave you unsupervised for a few months and this is how you spend your time, Trip?"

She shot a look at Dax. "Tell me someone dragged him off this ship and forced him to have fun occasionally."

Dax raised his hands. "We tried. Sometimes we succeeded."

Cris leaned back in his chair. "Hey now. I was busy. And thanks to the medi-bots, I don't need much sleep. I needed something to fill the hours, and this ship is not exactly a wonderland of entertainments." He didn't want to have this conversation again. Every member of the team had brought it up more than once. Even Nyx had suggested he might be pushing himself too hard, and she was a cyborg who needed even less sleep than he did and was currently studying multiple topics to fill the gaps in her education.

Aria nodded and sat back in her chair. "That explains why our medic is about to go undercover."

"Actually, that's not why he's on this mission." Dax glanced at him with something that might have been an apology in his eyes.

Cris sank a little lower in his chair. After all the work he'd done, he'd thought this was a promotion to a more active spot on the team. Apparently not. He'd been tapped because of who he'd been, not who he was now.

"I'm going in as someone of wealth and influence." It wasn't a question.

"You're the only one on the team who can handle this role, Trip. Nobody else has your upbringing, and those kinds of manners are hard to fake. Sabre couldn't do it, and that was just for a few hours at a party where all he had to do was shadow Colonel Archer. It has to be you."

"So, if blondie here is going in as a high roller, what's my role?" Aria tapped the edge of the table with two fingers. "And what's the op, anyway? Why all the secrecy, sir?"

Dax didn't answer her immediately. "Computer, activate all security firewalls for this room. And, Magi, quit eavesdropping on the briefing room!"

"I'm hurt you'd even suggest such a thing, sir. I'm currently at a training arena watching my wife take the local cyborgs to combat school."

Cris burst out laughing. "You are so busted."

"*Veth*. I thought that message went out on the main comm channel. Guess I walked into that one. Huh? Signing off. Nyx has some kind of twirly death stick she wants to hit me with."

Magi signed off, and the three of them shared a brief chuckle. Eric had always had a thing for dangerous women, but none of them could have imagined he'd end up married to a cyborg assassin. Love was strange.

Cris glanced over at Aria and amended his last thought. Love was *fraxxing* complicated.

"Now that we're alone, we can get on with the briefing." Dax set his hands on the table, the knuckles of his left hand pressed to the metal. "Everything you're about to hear is so far above top secret that only a handful of beings in the galaxy know the full details. The rest of the team won't be read in until the mission is underway. You'll understand why in a minute."

Cris leaned forward and gave the commander his full attention. One of the things he appreciated about Dax was that he wasn't a stickler for military protocol. When he got serious, it was best to listen carefully.

"Caldwell, some of this you're already aware of, but I need to bring Jessop up to speed."

Cris nodded and saw Aria do the same.

"Forensic teams managed to collect enough genetic material to confirm the identities of the bodies in the pods."

Aria leaned forward. "The ones from the hidden lab Sabre and Bobbi found when they went after the stolen vial of medi-bots? The one where I got blown to hell?"

"That's the one," Dax nodded. "One of the bodies was Absalom's. Further testing confirms he's the right age to be the original version."

"The *original* version?" Aria's fingers curled into loose fists. "How many do we think are out there?"

"At least a few. We have intel that someone hunted down and destroyed several other bio-jacked clones, the ones he was using as vessels for his digitized consciousness," Dax said.

"*Fraxxing* hell. How are we going to find the rest? And who is going after the vessels?" Aria wrinkled her nose. "That is a really disturbing word to use in this context."

"Buckle up. It's about to get worse," Cris said. He'd been part of the initial investigation of the remains and had been kept in the loop even after the *Malora* had moved on to other assignments.

"Worse?" Aria asked.

"Absalom was on Astek station during the events of the gala. While we were off chasing Lieutenant Clooney and the stolen medi-bots, Absalom was running around the station wearing a cloned copy of an analyst with an extremely high security clearance. He, or someone working for him, killed and cloned the victim and then took his place."

"They can do that now?" Aria asked.

"Apparently. But only if the body they're transferring into is bio-jacked with the right hardware. Absalom's cloned vessel was killed during the attack on Astek Station. Another of VIDA's synthetic forms was also destroyed at that time."

"Another one? How many does it have?" Aria scowled. "Are we facing a self-replicating enemy? How do we fight that?"

Dax looked grim. "The good news is that we are certain the original consciousness of Dr. Absalom is dead and gone. He had no place to move his consciousness after his body died. The corpse looks the same as the others we've found, nothing but empty memory space where his digital consciousness should be. He went... somewhere. But with no vessel to move into, that energy would disperse. Absalom is gone."

"Small mercies," Cris murmured.

"Indeed," Dax said. "He's gone. The bad news is that VIDA isn't. It was an AI before it had a physical form. It can copy itself repeatedly."

Aria chimed in again. "Which must be how it was on Astek Station and on that jungle planet with us at the same time."

"Exactly. It can also exist in different forms—holo projections, digital avatars, as well as their synthetic bodies." Dax tapped the controls beneath his fingers, and a holographic display flickered to life in the air above the table.

Photographs and files of more than a dozen beings appeared in the projection. "We still have more bodies to identify, both at the facility we attended and more we've found since then. They're a mixture of doctors and scientists who have dropped off the radar lately along with corporate power brokers and CEOs, all listed as retired. Some of them are even registered as deceased."

Things fell into place for Cris. "That's our mission. Isn't it? We're going after VIDA."

Dax nodded once. "You are. I know you both have questions. I hold on to them for now. You need to see something first."

The files of the Gray Men and their accomplices vanished as a vid took over the space.

For a moment Cris thought he was looking at footage from their own interrogation rooms, but then Jemma Allen, the commander of Nova Force Team Four, stepped into the frame. She looked as cool and composed as always, her uniform crisp and not a hair out of place. The only indication anything was awry were a few tight lines at the corners of her mouth.

She went through the usual disclaimers about security clearances and classified intelligence warnings. Then the camera angle changed to show two other occupants, both of them seated across from Commander Allen.

Cris recognized both of them immediately. One of them was Master Sergeant Cleo Gottfried, the woman who had been Trinity's righthand officer when Trin ran Victor base, home of the Vault of the Fallen. Gottfried was in civilian clothes and she didn't hide what she was feeling. She was worried about something. Given she was seated next to a dead man, the source of her concern should have been obvious.

Only that couldn't be it... because she was holding his hand.

"Chad Everest is dead," Cris muttered. "I cleaned charred chunks of his gray matter off the bulkheads myself. I *know* he's dead."

"That is not Chad Everest," Dax said. "That's the last of Absalom's clones."

The interrogation was more of an interview. Allen started by asking Gottfried to identify herself.

Cleo gave her name and rank. Then, looking slightly downcast, she added the word, "retired."

Once that was done, she returned to her brisk, no-nonsense style and summarized the situation with minimal questions and prompting. It was obvious she'd been through this before. When she was done, Gottfried turned to the man beside her and Dax paused the vid.

"Questions?" their commander asked.

"Let me get this straight," Aria said. "Long ago, Gottfried had a love affair with the original Absalom. He left her as his obsession with VIDA and the Grey Men's agenda intensified. Instead of moving on with her life, Gottfried spent the rest of her time in the IAF posted to that same base on Ibix 4. Then, one day, out of the blue, he shows up at the base and she just... let him in? And then she somehow convinced him to turn himself over to Nova Force because she was once in love with another version of him?" That's the plot of a serial holo-vid like *As the Moons Rise.*

"I know, but their stories have been repeatedly vetted and verified. The clone, who has requested to be referred to as John, has provided us with a great deal of solid intel. All of it has checked out so far. We believe he is a reliable source." Dax winced slightly. "But as you might have guessed, some of the other members of this team are *not* going to be happy to learn where we're getting our intel from."

"No kidding," Aria drawled. "Considering the fact that several versions of that man and his rogue AI have attacked, imprisoned, and tried to kill various members of this team more than once."

Dante, Kurt, Eric and Nyx were not going to like it. Hell, Trinity and Dax couldn't be thrilled about it, either. Aria's hands closed into tight fists and she moved them out of sight beneath the table.

"If you'd like to withdraw from this mission, now would be the time to say so," Dax said. "Once you know much more, you're going to be in too deep to change your mind."

Aria shook her head sharply, but Cris managed to speak before she could. "I'm in. If it means ending this threat, it doesn't matter where the intel came from. If you trust it, I trust you, sir."

"Same here," Aria chimed in.

"Alright then." Dax rapped on the table twice. "Welcome to Operation Sunset. Here's what you need to know."

They reviewed the recordings of their source's interviews for more than an hour, getting the rest of the information they needed. By the time it was done, Cris's head was crammed full of facts and he suspected his eyes had the same glazed look Aria's did.

"Until we depart from Haven, none of what you've been told leaves this room. If you want to go over any of the information, I'll arrange for you to come here to review the single copy of the data we have. For obvious reasons, we can't risk putting this information anywhere it might end up accessible to VIDA or whoever it's reporting to now," Dax said.

"*If* it's reporting to anyone. Version one of that program went rogue already. Odds are good that this one has done the same thing." Aria leaned back from the table and rolled her shoulders, tipping her neck from side to side to loosen up the muscles.

Cris was almost overcome with the need to walk over and massage her neck for her, the way he'd done a few times before when the discomfort was greater than Aria's need to keep things professional.

Aria continued talking. "While the irony of Absalom's plans being foiled by his own creation is delicious, I'm not going to be able to enjoy it until we've put VIDA out of commission, too."

"If the clone—John—isn't lying to us, we know where it is and how to get to it. The only topic we haven't covered yet is our cover identities. Who are we going in as?" Crispin asked.

The holographic display shifted again to show Crispin's altered appearance on several identity cards and documents. "Caldwell, you're going as

Caspian Trace, designated agent for Tano Farr. Farr has a collection of agents working for him as freelancers, so no one will question why he has a new agent for this event. I'll send over detailed background files for both of you, but for now, all you need to know is that Trace is wealthy. He's also surprisingly well-connected through family links to a number of corporations and as mercenary as they come."

Dax flicked a finger and the image of Cris was replaced by another set of IDs but no picture. "Jessop, we'll add the images once you've seen Dr. Li and your appearance has been altered. You're going as Aspen Grove."

Aria snorted. "Caspian and Aspen? Seriously? Who is in charge of creating backstopped identities, and why haven't they been fired?"

Cris couldn't resist. "I don't know. I think Cas and Ass has a nice ring to it."

She shot him a look that made him want to grin and duck at the same time. "You would. So what am I supposed to be doing while big, blond, and buff is representing one of the most wanted arms dealers in the galaxy?" Aria asked.

Dax tapped the display to enlarge her file and pointed to the relevant information. "You're his bodyguard."

Cris rocked back in his seat. Dax might need him for this role, but the commander had just made it clear that despite all the work and training Cris had put in lately, the brass didn't think he was ready to go in alone. They were sending Aria to babysit him.

Of all the roles he'd cast Aria in over years of dreaming about her... babysitter was not on the list.

3

———

Aria left the briefing as soon as she was dismissed. She was going to need some quiet time to work through all the information she'd been given in the past hour.

Dax had requested Cris stay behind to discuss some administrative issue, so she'd made herself scarce. She was curious to know what they were talking about, but she'd find out eventually. Nothing stayed secret on this ship for long. With the amount of training Cris had done since she'd left, he was probably getting a raise. Maybe even a promotion. *Veth.* Was that it? Was he about to get promoted and transferred to another team?

Her stomach did a slow somersault that left her slightly nauseated. Would he leave? The logical part of her brain thought that might be the best option. She'd get to stay on the *Malora,* and Cris could forge a bright new future for himself with another Nova Force team.

The part of her unfamiliar with logic or common sense stomped around inside her skull like a Torski in combat boots, railing against the mere idea that he *might* leave.

She pinched the bridge of her nose and groaned softly. "I do not have time for this right now."

It had taken her weeks to come to grips with her new situation. She wasn't entirely human anymore. Accepting the ocular implant to replace the eye she'd lost in the line of duty had been an easy choice. The decision to accept the medi-bots, a combat-level cybernetic limb, and the extended contract she had to sign before they'd give her the upgrades had been far more difficult.

In the end, she decided to stay with the team. She'd made a promise to her parents that she'd see they got justice. That pledge had been the driving force of her life. She couldn't give up and retire until she'd fulfilled her promise. She might never know which of the Gray Men had ordered her parents' deaths, but that wouldn't matter if she took down the entire organization.

That was what she needed to focus on. Not her injuries, her implants, or her... she didn't know what Cris was to her anymore, but she'd figure that out later. For now, she had thinking to do, and the best place for her to do it was in the gym before the others got back.

She dropped by her cabin just long enough to change and then headed down a few decks to the *Malora's* fitness area.

The moment she stepped inside she noticed the changes. There was far more equipment here now, enough for the whole crew to work out at once instead of taking turns. The improvements made sense given the ship was their de facto base of operations and home for the time being. Not to mention the team had expanded more than once in the last year.

Space on board was tight. So, instead of expanding the size of the gym, someone had added grav-plates to the formerly bare walls. When activated, the altered gravity created more floor space. Resistance machines and treadmills of various types were now mounted to the walls, leaving room on the main floor for the sparring mats, heavy bags, and the free weights.

She'd heard about this kind of setup on a few ships but had never seen it herself. Curious, she warmed up quickly and then activated the grav-plates on one wall. Once all the lights showed green, she gave the wall a dubious glance and then walked cautiously into the gravity transition area.

Vertigo hit as her body registered two different directions as "down." Aria ignored it and kept moving, placing one foot on the wall and then locking her eyes on what had been the ceiling and then reorienting herself. It was the same thing she'd been taught to do when in zero-G training, and she'd gotten good at it over the years.

Once her dizziness faded, she risked a glance back at what had been the floor, but her brain continued to accept her new orientation without protest. Yeah, this would work nicely. Though she appreciated that the designers had left the free weights in their original places. If the grav-plates failed, no one would end up dropping their weights on an unsuspecting crewmate.

It didn't take long for the familiar routine of physical training to engage her body while leaving her mind free to focus on other things. They were going after the Gray Men... or what was left of them. If this mission succeeded, it might be the last nail in the Grays' collective coffin. That thought settled deep in her heart in the form of a warm glow. It was about time.

The mission wasn't going to be easy, though. Their only source of intel was John, a clone of one of the original masterminds of the whole organization. To say his information was suspect was like calling water wet.

Their intel revealed that the station where VIDA's software was housed was so secure there was not a snowball's chance in a supernova the rest of the team was going to get anywhere close. It had taken planning and luck to get even two operatives into Babylon Station. She and Cris were going to have to trust each other. She could do that. Trust had never been their problem. She'd trusted him from the moment they'd met. Maybe that's why it stung so much that he'd pulled away from her now. She'd trusted him—more than anyone else on the team. *Hell*, she'd let him past her walls and shared more of herself with him than anyone else in her life.

He was her friend. *Had* been her friend. *Fraxx*.

She shook her head and pushed her body harder, arms straining as she increased the resistance again. If their friendship had changed because of her injuries, she'd deal with it. She could understand the reasons. Her cybernetic eye was easy to overlook, but Cris had seen the damage to her leg and had to know how much of her wasn't human anymore.

Being born a cyborg was one thing. Becoming one later in life was something else. It had been hard enough for her to accept her new reality. She hadn't been sure how the rest of the team would feel about the changes... well, anyone but Nyx. The cyborg had been accepting and supportive from the moment Aria had woken up and discovered her life had changed.

This was a blessing, really. She'd lost friends before. Time and people moved on, situations changed, and sometimes people died. She'd deal with it. But if she hadn't pulled away from him after discovering they were going to be coworkers... this would have broken her heart. Keeping her distance had turned out to be the right choice, even if it hadn't been the easy one. In fact, she'd questioned her decision more than once, especially as other couples formed on board and within their team. Her rules for never mixing business and pleasure seemed arbitrary and stupid now that the rest of the team had paired up and were happily working with their partners.

Damn it, she really needed to let this go. She had to focus on the mission, not the state of her relationship with Cris. She'd been trying to get him to move on for years. She didn't have the right to be mad now he'd finally done it.

"I'm an idiot," she muttered and forced herself to think about something else.

The mission. VIDA's main system was housed in one of the most secure facilities in the known galaxy. Known to the humans as Babylon, the space station had the best of everything and catered to the richest beings in the galaxy. It had more security than most governments and offered itself as neutral territory to any group who could afford to pay for their services.

Wars had been ended there, alliances forged, and some of the most dangerous organizations on record kept their secrets stored in Babylon's legendary vaults. That's where VIDA was. They needed to get in, find the right vault, and deactivate the rogue AI for good. It wouldn't be easy, but if John's intel was right, it *was* possible.

And she had to admit, Cris's background made him perfect for this role. She knew he came from a family with more wealth and power than she could ever imagine. He'd be able to blend in with the beings there even though he hadn't been part of that world for a very long time.

She was still processing the changes he'd gone through since she'd seen him last. The new appearance was just part of it. She'd accessed the unsealed parts of his file while she changed clothes and perused the list of credits and training certifications he'd acquired lately. It was a jaw-dropping list. Had he slept at all while she been gone, or had he spent every waking minute on his mission of self-improvement? She suspected it was the latter. Why hadn't anyone else reminded him to take some time for himself? She couldn't be the only one watching over him. Could she? Sabre had to have known, and Dr. Li had been on board for weeks. No way could Tyra have watched him do this to himself without saying anything.

Even Dax had shown some concern at the beginning of today's briefing. She'd have to talk with the others and find out what was going on with Cris. Subtly, of course, otherwise they'd think it was a personal interest instead of a purely professional one.

They were going undercover together. If something was going on, she needed to be aware of it.

That's when she realized her thoughts had drifted back to Cris. *Again*. At least Shadow wasn't around to sense what she was feeling and give her one of those deep, meaningful looks the cyborg was so good at.

"Focus, Jessop," she scolded herself. "Or should that be focus, Aspen Grove?" She winced at the sound of her new name. Still, she'd get used to it. She always did.

Another twenty minutes of mental and physical exercise resulted in a pleasant endorphin high and a plan. She'd played mercenary types before. It wasn't that difficult, given her upbringing.

Both her mother and father had been military and done their service before cashing out to go private. It had been good, steady money, and they'd done it for years with minimal injuries and only a few close calls. At least, that's what she'd always believed.

Even after she'd joined up and left home, she'd thought they were safe enough.

She'd been wrong.

She was nineteen when it happened, a private in the Intergalactic Armed Forces, barely a year out of basic. Her parents had taken a job, gotten into a bad situation, and vanished. Their bodies had never been found.

Her own investigation into her parents' deaths had brought her to Nova Force's attention. She'd done it all on her own time, teaching herself what she needed to know along the way. When they'd offered her a job, she'd accepted it without hesitation, and soon she'd known more than she wanted to about what her parents had really been involved in.

For the year before they vanished, most of their contracts were for known members of a cabal now known as the Gray Men. She wanted to believe they didn't know who they were working for. They'd always been careful, taking the smaller, simpler jobs that paid less but had far better chances of success. Somehow, they'd been drawn into the web of dangerous deceits that were the hallmark of the Grays, and it had gotten them killed.

One day she'd get justice for them. Hell, if this new mission panned out, maybe that day would be soon.

Aria was just finishing up when Tyra entered the gym. "I thought I might find you here. Dante likes to hit the gym after going to a mission briefing. He says hit helps him think."

"Yeah, we usually work out together after a session." Aria secured the equipment she'd been using and sat up. Her inner ear protested and this time her stomach joined the fun. Now that someone was standing on the real floor, her senses were providing conflicting input on which direction was "down" again.

Tyra looked as queasy as she felt.

"One sec, I'll join you before both of us get space sick," Aria said.

"That would be appreciated. Though it's nice to know I'm not the only one it affects. Nico loves it, and I think the others all pretend it doesn't bother them when I'm around."

Aria moved toward Tyra, bracing herself for the transition point between the two gravities. Once they were on the same surface and her stomach had settled, she greeted the diminutive doctor with a hug.

"I can guess why you're here. Dax told you I was ready for mission prep. Didn't he?"

"He did. I thought I'd come by and see if you were free to start the preliminary workup. Most of the changes will be simple cosmetic alterations, enough to confuse facial recognition scans and make sure no one recognizes you."

"Yeah, I really don't need the ghosts of investigations past appearing and blowing my cover." Aria grabbed a towel from a nearby rack and dried the worst of the sweat from her face and neck. "Ready when you are."

~

Cris left the briefing room feeling a little dazed. He'd been promoted to lieutenant commander. Or he would be, if he accepted a transfer to another team. Jemma Allen had personally requested him for an open spot on her team. He'd been considering this for months, but now the opportunity had presented itself, he wasn't sure he wanted it.

"You don't need to make a decision until after this mission," Dax had told him. "If you decide that's what you want, I'll give you a glowing recommendation and let you go on your way." He'd tapped his knuckles against the table three times. "But I'd be lying if I said that's what I want to happen. We need you here, Caldwell, and I'm a selfish bastard who wants things to stay the way they are."

Cris wasn't sure that was possible. Not now. Not for him. Maybe he and Aria could find a way to work through their issues while they were on this op. *Maybe.*

If not... at least he had another option.

He'd intended to go back to his room and make plans for the mission. At the top of his list was the need to work out the details of his new persona. Some of his high society manners could reveal far too much if he wasn't careful. His accent alone would be enough to give away his planet of birth, education, and social status. He'd have to make adjustments and find ways to create uncertainty about who he was... or had been.

If this was any other mission, he could have talked to Aria about it—not only because they were teamed up for this op but because she was the one he'd always been able to talk to about anything. While he'd seen a few signs that their friendship hadn't crashed and cratered yet, he wasn't ready to talk to her about this... or about the potential promotion and transfer. He could reach out to his little sister, but he already knew what she'd say. She'd tell him he was overthinking things and to go with his gut. Which wasn't helpful since his lower intestines didn't know what to do either.

He was almost to his quarters when he had a moment of insight that brought him to a halt in the middle of the corridor.

"I'm an idiot," he announced to the empty air. "A total *fraxxing* idiot."

He'd spent a lot of time lately training both his body and his mind because he wanted to be sure he had options. The team didn't need his skills as a medic much anymore, so he'd made sure he had enough skills and abilities that he'd still be an asset. He'd taken control of matters and worked toward the outcome he wanted.

So why the hell was he letting go of Aria so easily? He'd respected her decision to call off their relationship because they worked together. At the time it had seemed like the right thing to do.

It didn't feel that way anymore.

When this mission was over, the two of them were going to talk. He might have to lock the door and tie her to a chair to make sure she stayed long enough to hear him out, but he'd been studying up on restraint techniques to use on cyborgs and other enhanced beings... he'd find a way.

He didn't get any farther in his planning before he got an incoming message from Dr. Li. One of the benefits of the medi-bot treatment was that it allowed them all to be implanted with internal comm devices. Something about healing speeds and the body's ability to accommodate implants. While they had limited range, the channel was encrypted and permanently linked to the other members of the team.

He answered, subvocalizing his response. "What can I do for you, Doctor?"

"Lieutenant, I could use your help in the med-bay. I've just finished the preliminary workup for Lieutenant Jessop's procedure and she has agreed to get it done today. It would go faster of you assisted me."

"The lieutenant isn't likely to want me there. Not after the last time we were in the med-bay together."

After a two-second pause, Tyra replied in a tone

that nearly crackled with tension. "Do you really think I would request your help with a patient without getting their permission first?"

Great. Now he'd insulted Tyra, one of the best doctors he knew. At least no one else could hear this conversation. "My apologies, Doctor. I shouldn't have made that assumption and I didn't mean to question your ethics." He could have left it there, but he felt he owed her more than that. "Your request surprised me and I misspoke. I will be there shortly."

"Thank you, Lieutenant." Tyra's tone softened. "And stop being so hard on yourself. No one could have done more than you did that day."

One day he might believe that, but it wouldn't be anytime soon.

He set aside all thoughts about the mission and focused on what Tyra would need from him. Most of the procedures would be simple ones: cosmetic alterations to Aria's appearance, fingerprints, and anything else that could give away her real identity. She'd also need her comm implant tuned to the team's encrypted channel. No one outside the team knew what it was, so there was no way she would have it done already.

Everything felt normal until he walked into the med-bay. The moment he saw Aria stretched out on the surgical table with her eyes closed and her body covered by a single blanket, he was thrown into the past... to the last time she'd been in this room.

She'd been unconscious that time, her dark skin ashy with her lips and palms tinted blue as her body struggled to stay alive despite the massive blood loss.

He'd worked desperately to stabilize her, giving her as many healing accelerants as he dared. It hadn't been enough. By the time he'd repaired the worst of her internal injuries, what was left of her mangled leg was beyond saving. He couldn't do anything but remove the pulverized flesh and splinters of bone that were all that was left of her limb.

He'd done what he had to—the only thing he *could* do in order to save her life—but it didn't make his choice any easier to live with.

The memory faded when Aria turned her head and opened her eyes as she smiled in greeting. "Hey. I was wondering when you'd show up."

The area around her was already bathed in the soft glow of the sterility field and the med-system's surgical unit was already in place above the bed. The results of various scans were displayed on the monitors. He scanned them automatically, some small part of him relaxing as he reassured himself that everything was normal. This wasn't like last time. There was no emergency. This was a simple set of procedures Aria had already agreed to.

He smiled and walked over to where she lay. "I'm getting into character. Only peons and underlings arrive on time. The rest wander in at carefully calculated times based on their wealth, influence, perceived importance, and their mood."

The field tingled slightly as he entered it, and he paused before getting too close, giving it time to eradicate anything that might endanger the patient. It only took a few seconds before it chirped to confirm he was in the clear.

"Ah, you're here!" Tyra called from the far side of the bay. "I'm nearly ready. If you could just entertain our patient for a few more minutes, I can get the rest of the instruments ready. Then we can begin."

"I can do the prep for you, Doctor."

Tyra snorted in amusement. She sounded a lot like Dante, and it was odd hearing the noise coming from the diminutive human woman instead of the hulking brute she'd fallen for. "I didn't ask you to assist just to get you to set up instruments for me. I'm going to need some hands-on help. I wasn't aware that the lieutenant had been given both types of nanotech. Her healing time may be even more accelerated than I was prepared for. This will go smoother if two of us are doing the work."

That was news to him, too. "Both kinds?" he asked, looking down at Aria.

She nodded. "It was Shadow's suggestion. Since someone is trying to mess with the Vardarians' version of the tech, she figured it wouldn't be long before someone did the same to the cyborgs and anyone else with medi-bots. This way I have some built-in backup."

"Backup. Right." He smirked. "So this was entirely a practical decision and had nothing to do with your competitive nature at all..."

"Nope. None at all." She grinned back at him. "That's my story and I'm sticking to it."

Banter and bickering with Aria was familiar territory. In fact, it was what he'd missed the most. This. Being with her. Teasing and laughing and finding a way to deal with whatever insanity the universe chucked their way.

He almost said that, but this wasn't the time or the place. He needed to focus on her right now. "Do you have any questions about the changes Dr. Li will be making?"

"We covered everything already. I'm good to go." She narrowed her eyes at him. "I also know exactly what the plan is, so if I wake up with three boobs, I'm blaming you."

"Three? I was actually thinking four." He held up his hands to his own chest and made a juggling motion. "Symmetry is important, and that way you're still well-balanced up front. But if you're sure..."

"Doc, you heard that. Right?"

"I did. Not to worry, I'll make sure he doesn't get anywhere near that part of your anatomy," Tyra replied.

"Thank you," Aria said then stuck her tongue out at him. "Jerk."

"That's Lieutenant Jerk to you."

"I said entertain the patient, not get her all riled up," Tyra said as she stepped into the sterile field with an injector in her hand.

Aria took a deep breath and then nodded. "As ready as I'll ever be."

"I'll be here when you wake up." The words came automatically. It was the same thing he said every time he had to put one of his teammates under. And he always had... Until Aria's surgery. Dax had ordered him to get some rest and he'd done that instead of staying to be there when she woke. He should have stayed, but if he was honest with himself, he hadn't wanted to face her when she learned what he'd done.

"You weren't last time." Aria said with an accusatory undertone.

"Last time was different," he said. And wasn't that the understatement of the century.

She didn't say anything else, and within minutes she was unconscious. They started the procedure. His primary job was to keep an eye on the scans to make sure nothing surprising was going on and do a few of the simpler alterations.

The scans revealed some surprises. For one thing, it was quickly apparent that Aria had far more cybernetic enhancements than he'd expected.

Someone had implanted neural enhancers and artificial muscle fibers in her non-cybernetic leg. It was woven it in with the organic material in order to increase her strength and speed so she could run without tearing herself apart. Her ocular implant had also been updated, and it looked like she had a Vardarian comm unit implanted, one with a translation capacity the rest of them did not have.

She had to have agreed to each upgrade, which meant he wasn't the only one who had been looking for every advantage when it came to the fight against the Grays.

He looked down at his own forearm. The data port was hidden by the sleeve of his uniform. He wasn't a fully jacked cyber-jockey, but he was on the bleeding edge of what regulations allowed. Eric was teaching him how to use it, and he was a fast learner.

It was one more thing Aria didn't know about. Would she understand his reasons? And why had she wanted him here? Was it so he could see for himself that she'd made choices, too. Or maybe this was her way of showing him what the accident had cost her.

Fraxx if he knew.

The two of them worked with efficiency, and within an hour the surgery was done. Dr. Li stepped back, her gaze still on Aria. "What do you think?"

"I think you missed your calling. You could be making a fortune doing black-market identity changes for the criminal underworld." The work Dr. Li had done was impressive. With deft touches and small changes, she had altered Aria's appearance sufficiently to fool any face or body scan.

Tyra beamed. "I'll take that as a compliment."

"You should. You do nice work, Doctor."

"So do you. If I had tried to do this alone, I'd still be working, which means I'd have to give the lieutenant another dose of anesthetic. I'm glad we could avoid that." Tyra nodded at him and then stepped out of the sterile field. "I need to clean up and then let Commander Rossi know we're done. If things go well, I imagine you'll be able to leave tomorrow."

"Would you like me to assist with the cleanup?"

Tyra shook her head. "No. You stay with her. With her nanotech I imagine she'll wake up very soon. You should be here when she does."

He looked down at Aria and felt the same familiar pang of longing he always had when he was close enough to touch her... but couldn't. "Yeah, I should."

He deactivated the sterile field and settled in to wait. If Aria wanted him to be here when she woke up, here is where he'd be.

He owed her that.

4

———

Several days later, Aria still couldn't pass a mirror without startling when she saw her reflection. Logically, she knew it was still her, but even after seeing the mockups, she hadn't expected to look so different. The issue was amplified by the fact she'd never been somewhere with so many reflective surfaces. Tano Farr, the notorious weapon dealer they were claiming to work for, clearly had vanity issues the size of a planet.

Tano's obsession with outward appearances probably explained the look Aria was now sporting. Tyra had opted to give her a makeover the doctor had called "alien chic." Her skin now had a metallic gold shimmer to it with a subtle scale pattern that made her look a bit like a Vardarian. Her eyes were Pheran silver now, and her dark, curly hair was gilded with streaks of metallic gold. The lines of her face had been altered, too. She had higher cheekbones, fuller lips, and semi-permanent make-up far more elaborate than anything she could have managed. She appreciated the make-up, but the whole thing

felt like she was in costume... one she couldn't take off at the end of the day.

At least Cris seemed to like her new look.

He'd been there when she woke up, just like he'd promised. She'd heard him humming to himself before she'd even opened her eyes. It had been comforting to know he was there. Maybe he was starting to accept the changes.

That would explain why he'd been around more since then. The *Malora* was big enough he could have vanished whenever they weren't working, but instead it had started to feel more like the old days. They joked and teased each other as if nothing had changed, both of them working hard to avoid talking about the Torski-sized issue that followed them around.

They hadn't had time, really, in an out of briefings and planning sessions since they'd left Haven colony. Even as big as the *Malora* was, not a lot of areas allowed for a private conversation, especially not when a cyber-jockey and cyborg assassin, both with enhanced hearing, were on the team.

Privacy wasn't an issue anymore, though. They were alone on one of Tano's private vessels. His recent arrest had been kept a secret, which allowed them to use his name in vain and even take temporary possession of the *Twisted Vixen*. Nova Team Two had taken down Farr less than a week ago, creating a brief window of time before his capture would be discovered. Hopefully she and Cris would be long gone before the news broke.

The *Vixen* was a fully automated vessel, a fact that had irked Cris when he'd first realized he had no reason to take over as pilot. He hadn't sulked for long, though. They had too much to do. They'd be arriving in less than twenty hours, which meant their last chance to get a decent night's sleep was tonight. Medi-bots or not, they were going to be pushed to their limits over the next few days. Babylon Station was a sanctuary for most of the guests there. For the two of them, it was hostile territory.

The infamous space station had different names in various languages, but they all referred to the same place. A luxurious station in a system just beyond Jeskyran space, it was outside the legal reach of any government signed on to the Unified Galactic Agreement. The station was run by a brood of Jeskyran males who had renounced citizenship and operated as an independent entity that was somehow legal under the laws of their species. Here, even the most notorious could show their face without fear of arrest, and the richest beings in the galaxy could store their riches—and their secrets. One of those secrets was the high-security vault that housed VIDA's original program. This would be the most difficult op of her career, and they were going in alone.

It made her all the more grateful she and Cris were on firmer ground right now. Right now, they needed to focus on putting an end to the VIDA before the damned AI figured out a way to end them. With no one left to hold its leash, it was only a matter of time.

Pushing that grim thought to the back of her mind, Aria left her lushly appointed cabin and made her way to the ship's main lounge. Every surface that wasn't reflective was covered in dark purple velvet, most of it trimmed with garish shades of red and gold. For all its overdone opulence, it wasn't very large, and most of its mass was dedicated to the engines, which were some of the fastest she'd ever seen. The living space wasn't much more than what a standard shuttle had to offer, so the fast travel time was a blessing. More than a day or two cooped up in here would have even the best of friends sick of each other's company.

They hadn't been on board long, though. The ship had made most of the trip on its own. A small change in its program had diverted it to an uninhabited system where it had rendezvoused with the *Malora*. Eric had come on board long enough to wipe the AI pilot's memory of the detour and alter its manifest to show it had never changed course and had certainly not met up with an IAF vessel to acquire two new passengers. As far as it knew, Caspian Trace and his bodyguard had come on board before the *Vixen* left its owner's private moon.

Cris was already in the main cabin when she got there. He had his feet up on a purple velvet footstool with his hands behind his head and his eyes closed. She wasn't fooled for a second. He was as keyed up as she was.

They'd both come aboard in nondescript clothing. She was still wearing hers, but Cris had changed into one of the outfits that went with his new identity. The vest he wore was definitely based on Vardarian fashions. It had a thick band of ornately decorated material around the collar with a single fastening near the top. The rest of the fabric fell away in an inverted V that left most of his chest and stomach bare.

Based on what she could see, her partner had spent some serious time in the gym. He'd always been fit, but his body type had always tended to the lean and athletic side. Not anymore. She hadn't expected the little stutter her heart made as she took it all in.

The bastard really did look good.

His outfit also showed off his broad shoulders and the hard lines of muscle in his arms, one of which now included something she knew had to be part of his cosmetic alterations.

"I see that Dr. Li went all out with your look, too. She gave you a fake data port and everything. I didn't realize Caspian was supposed to be jacked."

Cris's eyes snapped open. For a moment she was certain she read guilt in his expression, but he was too good at his job to let his emotions show for long. "Hey." He greeted her and dropped his arms as he sat up. "She did great work, but the data port wasn't part of it. It's real."

"Real? You had an actual port implanted for this? Why would you do that?" Not that she was opposed to upgrades, but Cris had never shown any interest in that sort of thing before, and the IAF didn't normally approve those kinds of things except for medical reasons like hers.

"It's not just for this mission. It's more job security. Magi has been teaching me how to navigate cyberspace and do some basic hacking. In our line of work, that kind of thing will come in handy at some point." He said it matter-of-factly, as if he hadn't just revealed he'd made major alterations to his body... and his *brain*.

She sank down in a chair opposite and fixed him with a disbelieving stare. "For *fraxx* sake. How many times do you need to hear this? You're not going to have to leave the team because we got medi-bots. You are more than just the guy who fixes our boo-boos."

"No," Cris said flatly, meeting her gaze for the first time. "I'm the guy who cut off my teammate's leg."

Well, *fraxx*. She'd assumed the tension between them was because she wasn't really human anymore. Years of training and experience as an interrogator and she'd forgotten two of the biggest rules in the business. Never assume a subject's motivations and never, ever let your own emotions cloud your judgment.

Double *fraxx*.

It took Cris a moment to register the words that had come out of his mouth. They hadn't been planned. Hell, he hadn't even known he was going to speak until it was too late.

So much for waiting until after the mission to hash out their problems.

It was Aria's fault for surprising him... and for looking so damned good. It was as if their time apart had weakened his control. This was more like it had been during their first few weeks together, when the chemistry between them had burned so hot it had been all he could do to respect the boundaries she'd set. He'd never managed to let it go completely, but he'd done what she asked and never crossed the line from friend to lover again.

But here they were, alone together, and he hadn't been able to concentrate on anything but her. The changes Dr. Li had made were stunning. He loved the new golden highlights on her dark skin and the way her black curls were now touched with gold. She'd changed her hairstyle while she was away. Now, the front of her hair was a tumble of curls that fell over one eye, though it was still cut short at the back and sides.

One day soon, he was going to give in to the temptation to touch her. They just needed to get through this mission first.

Aria stiffened, her expression a mixture of confusion, surprise, and dismay. "Is that what you think I think?" She scowled and shook her head. "Because that's not how I see it. You saved my life, Trip."

"By cutting off your leg," he repeated.

Aria laid her hand on the leg she'd had replaced. "I got a shiny new replacement. Which I will use to kick your well-sculpted ass if you ever say anything like that again. I wouldn't be here if you hadn't done what you did."

She frowned, her head tipping to one side as if something had just occurred to her. "*Fraxx.* Did I ever say thank you?"

Of all the things he'd expected her to ask, that hadn't even been on the list. "I don't remember. But given the circumstances, I wouldn't blame you if you hadn't."

She sat back in her chair and scowled, her fingers tapping out a rhythmic pattern on her thigh. It was one of her few tells, and it meant she was annoyed and heading toward furious at close to the speed of light. Any other day, he'd have taken the hint and changed the subject, but they were already in too deep for that to work.

"If I didn't say it, it would be because you didn't stick around long enough for me to get the words out. You ghosted me, you asshole. I thought..." she trailed off. The silence hung between them, but he resisted the urge to break it. He needed to get a better grasp on what was happening before he said something that sent this whole conversation into a tailspin.

Aria didn't speak. She didn't have to. Instead, she had dropped her walls and let him see more of herself than she'd ever shown him before. Hurt. Confusion. And beneath it all, a sense of uncertainty that was entirely unlike the gloriously confident woman he knew. She was one of the strongest people he'd ever met. What had happened to make her doubt herself?

The answer hit him like a rogue comet. *He* happened. Not when he'd made the choice to remove her leg but when he'd stayed away from her, thinking that was what she needed.

No wonder the rest of the team had been

wondering what was going on with him. He'd *fraxxed* up royally and hadn't even realized.

Aria still hadn't said anything. It was an interrogation tactic, one he was very familiar with. In fact, she'd taught it to him. Since he had no intention of jamming his other foot into his already crowded mouth, he tossed the grenade that was this conversation back to her again.

"Your turn. I already made my confession and got us into this minefield. You need to finish your last statement so we can find our way out again. What did you think when I pulled away?"

She managed to quirk one eyebrow while narrowing her eyes at the same time. "That is not how this works."

"I say it is. So, spill." Part of him wanted to keep bantering with her and put off any more talk about their feelings. It was easy and familiar and how he'd dealt with the frustration of being so close to the only woman he'd imagined a lifetime with.

"When the *fraxx* did you get this pushy?" she demanded.

He shot her a cocky grin he knew would annoy her. "I was left unsupervised." He tried to keep his tone light, but he didn't quite manage the truth that wrapped itself around the words. He'd missed her— her smile, her sarcasm, and the way she called him on his bullshit.

She nodded and sat up straighter. "Fine. Here's

the rest of it. When you ghosted me, I thought that meant we were done." Her lips quirked into a brief smile. "I mean, I've been telling you to move on for years now, but you never did. You've always been there for me, even when I didn't think I needed it. But this..." She gestured to her leg and then to her eye. "I'm not human anymore. I checked the percentages to be sure. I've got enough tech to be officially classified as a cyborg."

Cris opened his mouth to protest, but she cut him off with a raised hand. "Not that I'm accusing you of being biased. Your brothers-in-law are all cyborgs. I know that. But this feels different. I'm not the same person I was before. Hell, I'm not really a person at all."

"How did I miss it?" He managed to keep his tone light and conversational.

"Miss what?" Aria asked, clearly confused.

"The head injury. That's the only thing I can think of that would explain what you just said." He leaned forward to brush a hand over hers where it sat on her thigh. "As a trained medical professional, I can assure you that you are still a person." Until today, he would have stopped there, but his new plan meant ignoring the old boundaries she'd created. "In fact, you're a stunning female-type person, and I would totally hit on you if I didn't know you'd kick my 'well-sculpted ass' for trying it. Now you have the new leg, you'd probably break me in half if you did."

"I should never have said that about your ass," she muttered regretfully. "I don't suppose you'd allow a take-back on that one?"

"Nope. It's too late. I've even recorded it to permanent storage."

Her eyes widened at his statement, but instead of laughing, she looked concerned. "How much work did you have *done*? Isn't that risky? Hell, the last time I checked, the IAF brass wasn't too keen on any of their members getting cyber-jacked. Period."

"They're still not, but we're fighting battles on some very strange fronts these days, so they gave me the go ahead once I made my case. The Grays might be the first to use this technology, but we know once something is out there, it never disappears completely. Someone else will find a new way to use digitized consciousness or AI tech, and we'll be back here again. If the IAF doesn't adjust their strategy, we're going to lose this war."

"And you're the lunatic who volunteered to be the thin edge of the wedge." She eyed him speculatively. "And here I always thought you were the sensible one on the team."

"I ceded that position to Trinity."

"Clearly. This explains why Fido is sending me in as your bodyguard. He's realized you need a keeper."

That... actually made sense. It also took some of the sting out of their commander's decision.

"Bodyguard or not, I'm not going to hide behind your skirts if someone starts trouble."

Aria's brows shot up to her hairline as she raised one hand and extended her middle finger. "Point one. I do not wear skirts. My wardrobe for this mission is far more practical." She raised her index finger, turning the obscene gesture into something more mundane. "Point two. You will, in fact, stay back and let me handle any problems. That's my job. It's also my cover. The only one who gets to kick your ass for the next few days is me. We clear?"

"You mean my well-sculpted ass?"

She glared daggers at him. "I swear, I'm never giving you another compliment so long as we live. That was it."

"Then it's a good thing I have it archived," he shot back.

She threw back her head and laughed. He joined her, and in a matter of seconds, all the worry and guilt he'd felt for months fell away.

She was still snickering softly when he leaned forward and touched her hand again. The featherlight contact lasted only a second, but he needed her to hear what he was about to say. "I missed you."

She surprised him by catching his hand before he could pull away and giving it a quick squeeze. "I missed you too. Jerk."

"That's Lieutenant Jerk of the well-sculpted ass to you, Lieutenant Jessop of the dazzling silver eyes."

She flipped him off with both hands and got to her feet. "I need food. Want to see what this flying bordello has in the galley?"

His stomach rumbled as he got to his feet. The medi-bot treatment meant he had the metabolism of a teenager, even if he didn't need to eat nearly as often. The thought of good food still made him hungry, though. "You're on. I bet they have real steaks in the freezer. It's been a long time since I saw meat that didn't come from a vat."

Aria grinned, shoved him backward into his chair, and took off for the galley. "Last one there does the dishes!"

He didn't have a snowball's chance in a supernova of beating her there, so he stayed where he was and indulged himself by watching her ass as she ran. They were back on solid ground now, and that was a damned good start.

By the time they were done with this mission, he intended to have a plan to take their relationship out of the friend zone and into new territory. First, they had to survive Operation Sunset. Then he'd embark on his personal mission—the one that ended his time in the friend zone.

5

Aria started noting the differences the moment she stepped off the *Vixen*. Babylon was like no other station she'd ever been on. It was quieter for one thing, and the air was pure and lightly scented in a way that reminded her of the mountain breezes of Haven. The *Vixen's* air recycling system was good, but the station's was the best she'd ever encountered. Given she'd spent most of her adult life in space, that was saying something.

Cris finished locking down their ship before joining her. It would be under biometric lockdown and the onboard AI was programmed to alert them if anyone or anything happened in the ship's vicinity. The *Vixen* was their only way off the station. The *Malora* was cloaked and waiting for them at the boundary, but if it crossed over, they'd be operating outside their jurisdiction, which would trigger all sorts of problems if they got caught. This entire operation was off the books and existed in the murky middle of intergalactic law. They weren't infiltrating another species' territory, and the mission was to terminate a program, not a living being. Technically, they weren't breaking any laws.

Technically.

They'd been scanned and cleared for docking without any trouble. The next test would be to pass through security screening. Only, she didn't see anything like that. In fact, this section of the docking ring was empty except for the two of them and a small greeting party at the top of the passageway. They left their luggage for the service droids to bring up and went to find out what came next.

A Torski the size of a small mountain stood off to one side while two others, a female Pheran and a male human were waiting in the middle of the corridor with welcoming expressions. All three wore well-tailored uniforms of basic black trimmed with red.

The human male approached her and the Pheran made straight for Cris. They were both graceful and attractive. In fact, the male looked more like an actor or a model than anything else, and the Pheran was a classic beauty, her blue-striped features set off nicely by her black uniform, which also managed to show off her slender form to perfection.

"Welcome to Babylon Station," both staffers said

in perfect sync and offered them warm smiles as they presented her and Cris with identical monogrammed bags.

The male introduced himself to her. "My name is Ramon. With your permission, I would like to attach and activate your wristband. This will identify you and give you access to all areas you are approved to visit. Please do not remove it while on board. Without it, the system will not recognize you as a guest and could trigger automated security protocols. When that happens, the results can be... unfortunate."

"The wristbands weren't mentioned in our briefing," she sent to Cris. They'd have to find a workaround before implementing their plan.

"We'll figure it out," Crispin sent back.

Ramon continued speaking, his voice deep and sensual as he explained how the band worked. When he attached it, his fingers brushed her skin in a barely-there caress that triggered an unexpected rush of blood to her cheeks and made her pulse jump.

Odd. She glanced at Cris. He was watching the Pheran fasten another band around his own wrist. A quick scan with her cybernetic eye confirmed what she suspected. His body temperature had risen, and he was slightly flushed. They were having similar reactions... but to what?

"There," Ramon said as he finished his task. "Your room number has been programmed into your wrist band. If you tap it twice, it will call up a holo-map of the station. Contact me if you have any needs going unfulfilled. It would be my pleasure to ensure you have all you require during your stay. All you have to do is tap the band three times and speak my name," Ramon said with a sizzling look that added another degree to her body temperature. What was causing it? Because whatever it was, it wasn't Ramon. As pretty as he was, he was not her type.

"Thank you, Ramon. I am looking forward to our stay."

He stepped back just as the Pheran smiled up at Cris. "If you need anything at all, please feel free to call on me at any time. Just tap the band three times and say my name."

Cris nodded. "I appreciate the offer."

Aria switched to their internal channel. *"They're not much for subtlety. Are they?"*

"Not even a little bit. I think our medi-bots are protecting us from the full impact of the pheromones."

Pheromones. Of course. That kind of manipulation was illegal elsewhere, but Babylon was an exception to every rule, and clearly they took advantage of that any way they could. While naturally occurring pheromones wouldn't trigger a nanotech defense, these would be artificial, and even if she hadn't been aware of it, her medi-bots were. *"I wonder what other tricks they use on their guests."*

"We'll find out soon enough. Looks like we're in," Cris sent back.

Sure enough, their liaisons had stepped back and both were gesturing for them to continue along the passageway.

"Have a pleasurable stay," Ramon said as she passed him.

The Pheran, whose name she hadn't caught, nodded and smiled at them both. It disturbed Aria to know that if they were called upon, these beings would do anything asked of them. Who ended up working somewhere like this, and why would they stay? It wasn't part of the mission, but if she could find out more about this place and the beings who worked here, she would.

They reached the end of the passageway and passed through what the signs claimed was a decontamination field. A quick scan with her implant confirmed that was part of it, but most of the scanning was to confirm their identities and check for restricted weapons and contraband.

Once through the shimmering barrier, she realized it had also acted as a sound dampening field. The air filled with the soft murmur of voices, the tiny sounds beings made as they moved, and the unexpected sound of falling water.

Cris tapped her arm and then pointed to a waterfall cascading down one wall to fall into a pool of crystal blue water. "Is that real? Judging by the moisture in the air, I'd say it is."

She scanned it. "It's real. The falls, the pool, even the river. Some of the plants, too." The aquatic display was technically a river, though this one had been manipulated by grav-plates so it flowed in three dimensions. They both stopped walking to trace the path of the water. It wound its way through what she assumed was the main lobby to eventually make it back to the top of the waterfall and start the journey again.

"That's quite something," Cris said.

"And a hell of a mess if the power fails," Aria muttered. "Let's try to avoid walking under the big ribbon of gravitationally challenged water. Drowning on a space station is not how I plan to go out."

He shot her a sidelong look, and for a moment the emotion in his gaze made her forget how to breathe. He hadn't looked at her that way in—*veth*. He'd never looked at her that way before.

"You might be my bodyguard, but I'd never let anything happen to you, Aria. Never." His words sounded in her head, the private link making the statement feel like an intimate confession. Her first instinct was to push back at him. To remind him about the boundaries they'd agreed to. Well, he'd never really agreed to them. She just hadn't given him any other choice.

Flustered and caught up in an unexpected whirl of emotions, Aria did the only thing she could think of. She changed the subject. *"Can you die from an overdose of pretension? Because nearly everyone here seems to have a terminal case."*

The staff were easy to identify as they all wore variations of the same black uniform with red trim. They were the most understated outfits on display. Everywhere she looked beings were decked out in the latest fashions crafted from the most expensive of materials. It was easy to determine who the major players were. Each one was surrounded by their own solar system of aides and hangers on.

Crispin shot her an amused glance but didn't comment on the sudden conversational tangent. *"They must have learned to live with their condition. I suspect they cope by living in luxury with a steady diet of rare foods and age-extending treatments."* He paused and then surprised her by adding. *"At least, that's how my parents deal with it."*

He almost never mentioned his family. He'd distanced himself from them years ago, and he'd only reconnected with his sister recently.

"Do you miss it?" she asked as they made their way through the lobby toward the mag-levs that would take them to their assigned rooms. The ceiling was vaulted and reached stories overhead to reveal a view of the planet through the glass that enclosed the top of the lobby. Much of the planet was covered in

ice with bands of green and liquid water only appearing around the equator. As the station orbited the planet, the dazzling colors shifted through the spectrum. It was breathtakingly beautiful.

"*This?*" He gave a vague wave of his hand to encompass their surroundings. "*Not at all.*"

"*None of it?*" She didn't believe that. "*Surely you miss something about living this way.*"

"*The food,*" he admitted after a moment's consideration. "*Have you ever had real chocolate? It's incredible.*"

As they walked, Aria continued to scan and collect data on the area. The gravity was set to slightly less than standard, which meant that all the guests would be reasonably comfortable no matter what gravity they were used to. The interior was tastefully and surprisingly understated. The walls were sandstone in subtle bands of various cream shades with no bold colors or advertising to be seen. Balconies overlooked the central area, giving various elevated views of the three-dimensional river from above while the dark metal railings created intricate patterns when viewed from below.

"*I thought the Terran cocoa plant was extinct?*" she said, picking up the threads of their conversation.

"*Almost. A few sources are still left, though, if you have the money and connections to find them.*"

As they neared the lifts, Aria tapped her wristband twice and brought up a holo-map. Now she had this area scanned, she'd start working on the surrounding areas. They needed to work out multiple routes to their primary target—the holographic botanical garden exhibit they were told hid the access to the lower levels and the vaults. All they had from their source were descriptions from the one time he'd been here. Like everything else about Babylon, blueprints and even basic visitor maps were closely guarded secrets.

No botanical garden was on the map. *Fraxx.* She checked again and then ran a keyword search. Nothing.

Cris talked as she scanned, his demeanor that of an employer giving his staff an update. "The event begins tonight. Cocktails and first looks at the items up for auction. Then it's locked away again until the main event tomorrow afternoon."

The auction was their cover. Their supposed employer was a collector of art in all its forms and often sent agents to events like this to expand his collection. Aria didn't understand the need to spend the budgets of entire planets on something that had no practical use. Not that she was opposed to art and beauty, but the scrip spent on them could have permanently lifted entire populations out of poverty.

"Yes, sir. I'll be ready," she said, most of her focus still on the map.

"Of course you will, Ms. Grove. That's what I pay you for."

She noticed a chill note in his voice he'd never used before—not quite disdain but a close cousin.

She glanced up. Another group had come within earshot as they waited for their turn for the mag-lev. That explained it. She closed the map and shifted into her role as a bodyguard.

"You are in the Carina Suite in the Terra wing, sir. Once I've cleared the space, I will leave you to get settled."

"Thank you, Ms. Grove."

They made the rest of the trip in silence, but Aria's mind was in overdrive as they made their way to Cris's suite. If they couldn't find a garden exhibit, how the fraxx were they going to get access to the lower levels? While they had every right to be in the public areas, their wristbands would be a liability if they had to go poking into secured areas. The plan had been to remove them only once they were ready to make their move against VIDA.

They arrived at his suite and he opened the door by touching his hand to the palm scanner.

Once inside, they went through the standard procedures to ensure no listening devices or surveillance was in the room.

Once they were certain the room was secure, Cris turned to her. "What's wrong?"

"Our intel is out of date. There's no botanical garden exhibit. There are theaters, restaurants, sim-suites galore, and an entire level tagged as "Catered

Fantasies" that I am really hoping is not somewhere we need to search. Oh, and get this, there's a zoo here."

Cris blinked. "A zoo? On a space station?"

"Apparently it's mostly holographic, but some of the animals are real, yeah."

"Is it the newest exhibit?" Cris asked.

"Looks like it." She got his point. "So they've replaced the garden with a zoo. That's going to be a problem. We'll have to start our search there."

"Good thing one of us can see through holograms. You're our only hope of finding that accessway now."

"No pressure," she deadpanned. Only then did she take a look around the suite with a more casual eye. "You realize this place is bigger than every berth on our ship put together?"

"I think we could throw in half the gym, too. You should see my bedroom."

Aria snorted. "That line won't work twice, Trip."

He winked at her. "I had to try." She couldn't believe they were having this conversation. They didn't talk about that night.

"It's a lot of room for one person. If my place is smaller, I might just camp on your couch."

He raised a blond brow. "Dax didn't tell you?"

"Tell me what?"

"This is *our* suite." He pointed to the bedroom she'd checked out a few minutes ago. That's yours.

I'd be a gentleman and give you the master suite, but I'm supposed to be your boss."

"Why are we in the same room?" she demanded.

The bastard managed to look smugly amused despite the droll tone to his next words. "I'd assume it's because you're my bodyguard. You can't guard this body if you're not close to it."

"I don't know if I'm more annoyed with the fact that's actually a logical answer or the way you made it sound like a cheap come-on."

His aqua eyes flashed and the next thing she knew he was standing right in front of her, close enough she could smell the subtle spice of the soap he'd used. "If I come on to you, it won't be with a bad line and a wink. You're worthy of so much more than that."

Who was this man and what had he done with her best friend? Her pulse raced and she had to fight the urge to move. She didn't let herself dwell on the question of which way she'd go. Something told her she was as likely to step into his arms as to put some space between them. *Fraxx.*

The first coherent words she managed were a definite challenge. "I thought the point of all your work while I was gone was to make sure you were ready for anything. You don't need a bodyguard, Trip. You don't need me."

They stood there with their gazes locked. The air almost crackled with the tension between them.

Something was changing—had changed already—and she didn't know what to do about it.

"That's where you're wrong, Aria. I *do* need you. I can take care of myself, yes. But if shit goes sideways, I only trust one person to always have my back. You."

What the hell was he doing? This wasn't part of his plan. They were on a mission, for *fraxx* sake. Now was not the time for this. Cris knew that, but he couldn't seem to stop himself.

Aria reared back and for a spit-second, he thought she might be about to slap him. Instead, she threw her hands in the air and stormed away. "Now? You're doing this now? What the *fraxx* is wrong with you?"

That was a good question. "I honestly don't know," he admitted.

She spun around to glare at him, but her new eye color softened the impact somehow. He found himself missing her dark-brown gaze. The silver eyes were pretty, but they weren't hers.

He hoped she kept the new outfits, though. After years of seeing her mostly in either her uniform or workout gear, his libido enthusiastically approved of her current look. She wore a black and gold cat-suit that hugged her curves so snugly he was almost envious. She had on thigh-high boots of some glossy black material and a matching belt that hung low on her hips, complete with a stun-baton, one of the few weapons permitted on the station.

"Is this because you're feeling guilty again?" she demanded.

"No. This is..." he grunted in frustration. "Probably not the time, huh?"

That made her laugh. "You think?"

"Not unless I have to." It was an old joke, but it would help ease the tension. They needed to focus on the mission... and finding the damned access door.

She rolled her eyes. "You need new material."

"So you keep telling me."

Aria glanced over her shoulder to look at her bedroom. "We're tabling this discussion. I'm still absorbing the idea that we're sharing a suite. You, me. Same place, different bedrooms. I'm going to kill Fido when we get back. He didn't tell me. He just said my room was across the way from yours."

He couldn't resist pointing to her bedroom on one side of the suite and then to his on the other. "He didn't lie."

She scowled. "I'm still kicking his ass. Why wouldn't he just tell me?"

Cris suspected they both knew the answer to that. He wasn't going to be the one to say it aloud, though. If their commander was throwing them together to make them sort their shit out, then so be it. So far, it was working. "Worry about that later. Our luggage should be delivered any moment."

He shifted roles, altering his stance and expression to become Caspian Trace, a persona that was uncomfortably close to the man his father had wanted him to become. "After that, I suggest we take a stroll through the station. I have a sudden yearning to visit a zoo."

"It's uncanny how well you do that," Aria murmured and then nodded sharply and gave him a professional smile. "Of course, sir."

He walked over to one of the couches and settled into it to await the delivery of their luggage. They were back to playing their assigned roles for now. Later, though... Aria hadn't pushed back on what he'd said. She'd only protested about the timing. He took that as a good sign.

6

____

IT DIDN'T TAKE LONG for them to unpack their things and get settled. They were both traveling light, and even Cris's more extensive wardrobe didn't take long to put away. They could have handed the task off to the veritable army of bots and droids the station utilized, but they had changed the room's permissions to deny access to everything except for the housekeeping bots, and they were only permitted entry during certain hours. It was bad enough they'd be watched and likely recorded outside their suite. There was no reason to invite recording devices into their rooms as well.

They met in the main seating area between their two rooms to go over the plan one more time. To his surprise, Aria brought out her gift bag and dumped the contents on the table before sitting down and pointing to it.

"What is this?" she asked. "I mean, I know what it is, but why would anyone hand out this much stuff to people who clearly don't need it?"

Cris eyed the pile of complimentary gifts and shrugged. "Because it's the way this works. The more you have, the more you get."

"It's insane," Aria stated, her voice edged with disgust. "I mean, I know the whole system is corrupt and crazy, but this?" She picked up a crystal jar of spiced *Actari* nectar, an intoxicant luxury legendary for its pleasure-enhancing qualities. Several packets of real chocolate were included, along with a variety of other rare delicacies from across the known galaxy.

"I know," he said. The larger items included a high-quality communication device, no doubt loaded with spyware and other data-stealing abilities, and a top-of-the-line data tablet detailed with what looked like precious metals. Along with the various gifts were the usual complimentary gambling chips that could be used in the station's casino and an assortment of other items.

Aria wasn't done. "Do you realize that the contents of just one of these bags could pay for food for a family for a year on Earth? And would keep a family for months on one of the better colonies."

He nodded. He knew. It was one of the reasons he'd joined Nova Force. "Why do you think I left this life behind?"

She paused, her expression softening to one of thoughtful consideration. "I thought you were escaping your parents' control."

She wasn't wrong, but there was so much more to it than that. He gestured around them. "I hated it. Hated this. So did my sister. And whatever I say or do over the next few days, please remember that this is all just an act and isn't who I really am."

Silence fell between them, and her thoughtful look intensified. He knew she was reading more than just his expression. Aria was a gifted interrogator who could read body language better than anyone he knew, and right now she was using all of her skills to unpack his past statement.

He let her.

When she sat back and nodded, he waited, curious to hear what she said next.

"I didn't see the big picture. I'm sorry. I should have. Of course this isn't who you are." She blew out a breath. "You're going to hate this. Aren't you?"

He nodded. "Pretty much, yeah. But now I'm here, I understand why Dax wanted me for this role. I still don't like it, but I get it."

"You really grew up like this?" she asked.

"I did. Now you see why I left."

"I think so, yeah. You just never talk about it."

"For a damned good reason." He nodded toward the treasure trove of gifts on the table. "It's embarrassing to admit I spent the first half of my life sucking on a silver spoon." He didn't like thinking about this part of his past. And playing this role reminded him of who his father had wanted him to be. That was a version of himself he'd never wanted to meet.

He rose, crisply tugging at the edge of his new outfit. "Shall we go check out the zoo?"

Aria eyed him in amusement. "Seriously? You changed clothes again?"

He looked down at his blue vest with gold trim over wide gold trousers, and then back up at Aria. He struck a pose and said, "Welcome to the show. Brace yourself, Blink. From here on out everything you experience is going to be nothing but dazzling displays of ego, privilege, and wealth on a nauseating scale."

"Lovely. I can't wait," she deadpanned, and gestured for the door. "At your pleasure, Mr. Trace."

He nodded. "Thank you, Ms. Grove." Then he switched to their internal link. *"Later tonight, you'll have to try that chocolate. It really is incredible. The rest of the stuff we can donate once we're out of this lunatic asylum. I can think of a few families still recovering from the loss of Astek station that could use the help. We could send it all to my sister."*

Aria touched his shoulder gently. *"I like that idea."*

He didn't say anything, but he did reach up to cover her hand with his for a brief moment before he moved out. When she didn't pull her hand away from his, he grinned, though he was careful to look straight ahead so she couldn't see his smile. He was making progress.

He made a leisurely tour through the station with Aria watching his back every step of the way. He stopped at all the usual spots a first-time visitor might be drawn to. They viewed the lobby and its floating river from various vantage points, paused to refresh themselves with complimentary drinks from a cocktail and juice bar, and even passed through the casino on their way to the zoo.

A *zoo*.

Even after all the vainglorious and over-the-top displays of wealth he'd seen in his life, the idea of a zoo on a space-station was difficult to wrap his head around. Small holographic displays were common enough, but from what he'd read in the brochure, this was something far more elaborate. Not only were the simulations on a massive scale, but a surprising number of living creatures were mixed in with the holograms. The cost to transport and maintain the animals staggered even his imagination, and his father ruled half a planet.

They crossed through the lobby once more and took another mag-lev to the lower levels, where a myriad of entertainments was on offer. The zoo was easy to find. It was clearly marked on all the maps and took up almost the entire level.

It was a short walk across an ornately decorated foyer to the zoo's entrance, which was marked by a set of gates that reminded him of pictures of zoos he'd seen in children's books growing up. Faux brickwork and wood formed a large archway with a sign hung beneath it that said simply "Welcome to the Babylon Zoo." Around the gates were signs posted in multiple languages describing what to expect. There were warnings, too, along with a large map of the area and a downloadable program that would act as a virtual tour guide. They skipped the guided tour and set out on their own.

Without any reference points, all they could do was work their way through every exhibit. All their source's information had been related to details of the botanical garden exhibit they speculated the zoo had replaced. The only thing they knew was that the doorway would still be part of the station's physical structure, which meant it should be on one of the zoo's walls... somewhere.

Cameras and security bots were everywhere, which meant a direct approach would likely be flagged as suspicious. Instead, he wandered without a plan, casually pausing at any exhibit that caught his interest.

Any other time, he would have enjoyed the stroll. The exhibits were fascinating.

Some of the creatures they came across were familiar while others he had never heard of. A few weren't even carbon-based, though Aria confirmed that all those on display were holographic. Apparently even Babylon's budget had limits.

The design of the zoo made their search more challenging. Many of the displays had physical walls that kept visitors channeled into specific areas, and there was enough real greenery to limit Aria's ability to scan for their target. They had to keep moving, searching every possible area one at a time.

"This is taking too long," Aria sent along their internal link.

"Suggestions?" he replied.

"Time to switch to the observation areas? We've been here long enough the shift wouldn't be obvious."

He turned to her and spoke aloud. "I think I've had about enough for one day, Ms. Grove. I'm going up to the observation level to see if I notice anything I might want to visit tomorrow."

"Yes, sir." She inclined her head and fell in behind him once more.

It turned out that some of the exhibits were so large the only way to view them properly was from the upper levels. They found themselves standing above a stretch of open plain that looked like some sort of purple-grassed tundra, complete with a small running stream and holograms projected onto the walls to make the space look even larger.

Below him stood four massive beasts he'd only seen in vids until now—Nantari rhinos.

He'd assumed they were all holograms until he read the posted information. Two of the animals were real. They had three horns running down the centers of their massive heads, each one longer than his forearm and rising to a sharp point. They had to weigh over a ton each. They had mottled grayish-brown skin that looked like it could stop bullets, and all six of their legs were thick, muscular, and ended in a three-toed foot with massive claws.

They were temperamental, dangerous animals, and he couldn't believe two of them were eating from a feeder not ten meters below where he stood. While he watched the animals, Aria did a scan of the area, using their new vantage point to check areas she hadn't been able to see before.

After a few minutes, she gave a soft grunt of displeasure and her voice sounded inside his head. "*I have bad news.*"

He turned his back on the exhibit and leaned back against the railing. "Problem, Ms. Grove?"

"You're too close to the edge, sir."

It wasn't easy to hold two conversations at once, but he could manage it for short periods. Via their internal link he said. "*Please tell me the door we need to find is not inside the rhinos' enclosure.*"

"I trust the operators of this fine station to have measures in place to make sure their guests aren't devoured by the wildlife." He said and gave an airy wave of his hand. "They wouldn't be in business long if they didn't."

Aria kept her expression neutral and nodded once. "As you say, sir."

Internally he heard, *"The situation isn't quite that challenging, but it's close. It's located against the far wall of what appears to be a predatory fish display."*

That was going to be a problem. Their source had been inside the vault, but he'd been with the original Absalom at the time. He didn't have the access code for the door, so Cris would have to hack it. And that area was too open for his liking.

"Perhaps you'd like to include the aquatic zone in tomorrow's tour, Mr. Trace?" she suggested.

"Indeed. I have always had a deep fascination with sharks and the like." He nodded as if the suggestion appealed to him and continued their internal conversation. *"They have an aquarium. Here. Is it real?"*

"It's real." They took a moment to marvel at the audacity of this place. Then he turned back to gesture at the rhino, as if they were discussing it and not the other area.

"Remarkable, isn't it? I never thought I'd see a real one this close. Do put the aquatic area on tomorrow's agenda. I could use some practice staring down my fellow predators before tomorrow night's auction."

Aria's lips quirked slightly but she managed not to smile. "Of course, sir."

"*I assume at least some of the fish are alive, too?*" he sent to her.

"*Most of them are holographic, but not all of them.*"

He turned to face her again, making it look like he was deciding where to go next. "*How the hell do we get to it?*"

"*See the bridge? That appears to be the only way in.*"

The bridge she referred to was a walkway made entirely of glass or some other transparent material. It had high walls to ensure that the guests didn't end up going for an unplanned dip in the carnivore-filled water below.

It was also designed to be a security chokepoint with nothing to hide behind—no foliage or obstructions and multiple cameras focused on the area. No doubt the station would claim it was for the security of the patrons, but it was clear to him that it also protected the access door. He still couldn't see it, but he knew Aria could, and he trusted her. If she said it was there, that's where they needed to go.

He took another look at the bridge. Narrowing

his eyes as he recognized a familiar mechanism. *"How charming. I do believe that's retractable."*

She moved to the far side of the walkway to get a better look and then swore under her breath. *"You're right."*

"I'm ready to return to my room, Ms. Grove. We'll finish this tour tomorrow." He added via their link, *"We need to make plans."*

She nodded and said through their link. *"And whatever we do, we've already agreed there will be no drowning on a space station."*

"I'm making an addendum. No getting eaten by space fish either."

Before either of them could say anything more, things took a turn for the strange... and the dangerous.

The zoo used speakers to broadcast what Aria assumed were species appropriate noises through the various exhibits. She'd more or less tuned it out after a few minutes and only noticed when it suddenly stopped. A second of silence was followed by a cacophony of electronic screeching and static, the noise accompanied by a high-pitched whine that made her want to clap her hands over her ears to block it out.

The bone-piercing noise sent the animals—both

holographic and real—into a tizzy. Most bolted in blind panic and some tried to hide while others bellowed in fury and took up aggressive stances. She couldn't help but think that when they were programming the holograms, no one had considered what might happen in an emergency.

Someone was going to get fired.

The auditory assault made it hard to think, but she knew whatever was happening, it couldn't be good. They had to get out of here. *Now.*

Cris still stood against the railing, tensed and alert. Their eyes met in a moment of silent communication. Not that any other kind was possible at the moment.

That's when the rhinos charged the barrier. The holograms couldn't interact with the material, but the two real animals down there hit the wall with the force of a plasma grenade.

Metal shrieked in protest and the floor of the observation deck tilted. She heard the enraged bellows of the beasts in the pen below them and felt the thunder as they charged across the floor of their enclosure to slam into the wall again.

Struggling to keep her feet and figure out a way to get to safety, Aria barely noticed when the pattern of the static changed to a strange, distorted sort of babbling noise.

Cris had been thrown against the railing when the deck shifted. He was pulling himself hand-over-hand in an attempt to reach the still-stable part of the floor, so she rushed to help him.

It took her mere moments to undo her belt and secure it around one of the support posts. Then she caught hold of it in one hand and reached out for Cris with the other.

As their fingers brushed, the noise from the speaker changed again, becoming something almost human. It was distorted and wild, but it was definitely laughter. Cackling, maniacal laughter.

What the *fraxx* was happening?

Cris caught hold of her hand and grinned in relief. "Thank you," he shouted above the noise, but his words were drowned out by the laughter and gibberish pouring from the speakers. Words were buried in it now, random bits that didn't make any sense to Aria.

"Get you. Bitch. Open. Pay." At least, that's what she thought it was saying.

A resounding crash from somewhere below sent another shock wave through the floor and the deck Cris had been standing on collapsed into the rhinos' enclosure, leaving him dangling in midair with only her grip keeping him from falling.

If the impact didn't get him, the frenzied rhinos would.

"Don't let go!" she yelled through gritted teeth, hanging on to both him and the belt that tethered her to the still-stable part of the deck.

He looked into her eyes and grinned. "Never."

Then the lights went out and gravity vanished, leaving them both floating in the darkness.

Could this day get any worse?

She regretted the thought the moment it formed. Asking questions like that was just an open invitation to the universe, and she had more than enough to deal with right now.

At least the power outage put an end to the weird noise coming from the speakers. Now she could hear the angry snorts and turf-tearing claws of the rhinos as they pawed at the ground.

Cris caught hold of her forearm with his free hand and pulled himself toward her, which was easy enough to do now there was no gravity to deal with. Once he had his arms firmly locked around her waist, she pulled them back toward the safety of the stable area of the deck, careful not to tug too hard and send them flying off in some other direction. The way things were going, they'd end up in the *fraxxing* shark tank.

The emergency lights kicked on a few seconds later. They were floating less than a meter off the floor, but in the darkness she'd gotten disoriented and they'd rotated until they were almost horizontal with the deck.

That wouldn't have been a problem, but then an alarm sounded and the gravity returned, sending them crashing to the ground with Cris on top of her.

"Oof." All the air in her lungs came out in a whoosh.

"Nice catch," Cris said, his bigger body still pressing against hers.

"I'm going to pretend I planned it that way," she muttered. "You know, since I'm your bodyguard and all."

Instead of pushing himself off of her, Cris rolled them both over so that he was lying on the deck and she was sprawled across his chest, looking down at him.

"Better," he said.

"How is this an improvement?" she asked.

"Now I'm not crushing you." He reached up to touch her cheek. "You okay?"

"I will be once we're back on our feet." And once he stopped looking at her that way. His eyes were bright and his fingers traced lines of her face as he stared up at her.

She should move. It was the smart thing to do.
She didn't.

It felt like the most natural thing in the world when his hand slid into her hair to cup the back of her head. With the slightest bit of pressure, he drew her down to him. Her heart raced faster than ever and there was no point in pretending this was about the recent craziness. She knew this feeling. In fact, she'd been fighting it for years, and right now she couldn't remember why.

He whispered her name, their mouths so close she felt his breath against her lips as he spoke. Another moment and they'd be...

"Sir! Are you alright, sir? Do you need medical assistance?" Someone was running toward them, their light feet barely making any noise on the deck. Aria glanced up and spotted the little Pheran who had greeted Cris when they arrived.

Cris swore softly and turned to look at the new arrival. "I'm fine, Synda. Ms. Grove is capable of doing her job even if some others in Babylon's employ are not." His tone was harsh and nearly crackled with ice it was so cold.

She didn't like this version of him, not even as a persona. He moved into it too easily for it to be a new creation. This was something else—a person he'd been at one time. No wonder he'd chosen to leave that life behind.

More beings arrived, including Ramon, who offered her his hand as she got to her feet. She ignored him. She wasn't a damsel in distress. She was paid security to what they all believed was a rich and influential man. She helped Cris up, ignoring the way her arms and shoulders protested at this new abuse. She'd need a pain-blocker once they got back to their suite. Her lower limbs might be cybernetically enhanced, but her arms were just ordinary human tissue, and she'd pushed them to their limits holding on to Cris as he dangled above the rhino enclosure.

Once they were safely away from the damaged area, most of the beings focused on Cris, buzzing around him like annoying insects as they did their best to appease him and the other guests as they were gathered up and brought to the area around the main gate.

Apologies were plentiful, but explanations were in short supply. It didn't appear anyone was hiding what they knew. It was more that none of them had a clue what had happened and appeared as distressed as some of the guests.

Eventually Cris broke away from them with an angry slash of his hands. "Enough. Ms. Grove, with me. We're returning to my suite. There's no point in staying here any longer. Synda, I don't want to see you again until you have something useful to tell me."

"Of course, sir." Synda dropped her head and raised her hands in the Pheran gesture of supplication and obedience.

They were on the mag-lev a few minutes later. Neither of them spoke. The air of tension and anger continued until the door to their suite closed and Aria did a quick scan to confirm they were still free of surveillance.

They both sighed and looked at each other. "Are you doing the report on this, or am I?" she asked.

Cris groaned and dropped into the nearest chair with his arm over his eyes. "We'll do it together, but not until after we've both had a drink. I think we've earned one. Don't you?"

"I think we've earned two. At least," she agreed. "Along with a pain-blocker for me and some of that chocolate you told me about."

He dropped his hand and grinned at her. "Brilliant plan, Ms. Grove. Make it so."

She flipped him off before making for the food dispenser. Their medi-bots would neutralize the alcohol almost as fast as it hit their system, but that wouldn't stop her from drinking it anyway. It was a Nova Force tradition. Near-death experiences were always marked by a drink or two before writing up the report... and this one might be the strangest one she'd ever written.

7

____

Several hours later, Aria had a head full of questions and very few answers. It was part of the investigatory process, but it always left her feeling frustrated. She wouldn't relax until the answers started to fall into place—and given that their current goal was the destruction of VIDA, a task that had nothing to do with randomly occurring weirdness on board the station, the odds were good they'd never know what else was going on here.

But something *was* going on.

They'd both gone to their own rooms to shower, change, and organize up the first draft of their notes. Then they'd met in the main area to compare stories and compile the final report. Her ocular implant had recorded the entire event, which had helped confirm the timeline. They'd each recalled a few things slightly differently and some details one of them had noticed that the other hadn't, but the pieces fit together well enough. They knew what had happened, but not how, why, or who.

Why had the power fluctuated? What had caused the gravity to fail? Whose voice had they heard rambling amid the crackling static? She couldn't shake the feeling that it was familiar to her somehow. Had she come across that person before, or was it just her mind trying to create a pattern that wasn't really there?

It would take some time, but there was a chance the rest of their team would come up with some answers. Cris's upgrades couldn't handle more than thirty seconds of recording at a time, so he'd used his new implants to breach Babylon's systems and acquire a copy of the audio captured by the station's security system. They had included the audio and visual recordings with their report. Cris's cyber-jacked system was their only secure means of communicating with the *Malora* and her crew. They were too far apart for their internal links to work, and anything they sent out on the public channels was vulnerable to being hacked or traced.

Apparently Cris and Eric had set up a secondary communication system linked to their specialized hardware. She didn't understand the details, but it would somehow allow them to transfer data via cyberspace. The communication packets would be heavily encrypted and used several satellites and way stations to bounce the signal around before it would eventually make it to Eric. It wasn't the fastest system, but it was the most secure. If their cover was blown, it would be ugly, not just for them, but for all of Nova Force.

On top of security concerns and unanswered questions, another issue swirled around inside the crowded confines of Aria's skull. She'd almost kissed Cris.

What the hell had she been thinking? It went against every rule she had. Worse, it risked their cover. They weren't supposed to be lovers. She was supposed to be his bodyguard, not his... Whatever the hell that job title would be. Pleasure pet? Employee with benefits? Whatever it was called, it wasn't happening. It couldn't.

She kept repeating that to herself as she got ready. It didn't work. She knew it didn't because she took longer with her hair and make-up than usual. She wanted to look good. Not for the job, but for him.

I am out of my *fraxxing* mind.

She was his bodyguard, not his arm candy. Cris had seen her muddy, bloodied, and at her worst. There was no reason for her to be dressing up tonight to impress him.

But she had to admit, she did look good.

She still wasn't used to the gilded locks of hair or the strange patterns on her skin, but there was no denying it was attractive, if in a completely different way than she was used to. The clothes were her favorite part, though. She planned to hang on to the outfits after the mission ended. The bodysuits were more than they appeared to be and doubled as body armor—a sort of combat-catsuit that was as stylish as it was practical. Tonight she wore one that was a deep purple shade with lace insets that appeared to be light and filmy unless you examined them up close. They were actually made of woven metal and were as durable as the rest of her suit.

She tugged on her boots and then dropped a hand to her belt to check the position of her stun baton. Both belt and weapon had been retrieved and returned to her by one of the station's droids, along with a note of apology, a basket of pastries, a bottle of rare liquor from the Jeskyran home world, and another pair of gift bags, these even larger than the first.

The gifts were still piled on a table in the main room when she came out of her bedroom. Cris was already lounging on the couch, eyeing the stash with amusement.

"Imagine what they'd be sending if you'd actually gotten hurt," she said.

He glanced up and winked at her. "Let's not find out, hmm?"

She popped a piece of the chocolate into her mouth and barely managed to contain her groan of delight at the rich flavors and creamy texture. "For more of this chocolate I'd be willing to let someone rough you up a little."

"Remind me to look into hiring a new bodyguard after this stint. One that can't be bribed with chocolate." He got to his feet, giving her a chance to see his newest outfit.

Instead of the flowing fabrics and bared-armed look of earlier, he was now dressed in a perfectly tailored, black, *Keski* silk shirt that clung to his chest and shoulders like a jealous lover. Black pants and polished boots finished off the outfit, and to her mind, he looked like some sort of dashing pirate or a villain from one of the over-the-top historical holo-vids she sometimes indulged in.

Unable to resist, she grinned and asked, "Are we ready to set sail then, Captain Fancy-Pants?"

He grinned back and his next words were accompanied by a rich accent she'd never heard from him before. "Aye, lass. We are. It's time to see what treasures are on offer."

"That might be your best accent yet. You're just full of surprises, sir."

The look he shot her nearly made her trip over her own feet. It was dark and heated and full of something she didn't want to acknowledge. Not here. Not now.

"You have no idea, Ms. Grove."

He strode off without further comment, leaving

her scrambling to catch up. She fell into step behind him as they left the suite, both of them embracing their assumed personas.

They took the mag-lev down to the central lobby and crossed through part of the space, only to take another lift that brought them directly into the auction area. It was on the topmost floor of the station, and the private elevator hadn't started until they'd both held up their hands to allow their wrists bands to be scanned.

The trip only took a few seconds, but it felt as if they'd been transported to another world. The soft lighting and neutral décor were gone, replaced by a starkly elegant setting far less welcoming than other parts of the station. This was a place of business and power, and even the other guests spoke in hushed tones as they moved around the artwork on display.

The floor was gleaming white marble shot through with threads of black and silver. She had no doubt it was real stone, mined and transported at an expense large enough to bankrupt a planetary government. The entire ceiling was transparent, offering a view of the planet and the endless expanse of space beyond. Soft music played in the background, soft chimes and the airy notes of some sort of pipe or flute that were as cold as the vista that stretched overhead. Aria repressed the urge to shiver despite the warmth of the air. This felt more like diving into the waters of the shark tank they'd seen at the zoo.

"*Stay frosty,*" Cris said over their internal link.

"*That won't be difficult,*" she replied.

One corner of his mouth turned up slightly, but that was the only reaction he gave her.

Their welcome bags had included both a data packet and a physical brochure listing everything that would be available for bidding tonight. There were no images, though, and the descriptions had been vague and poetic, leaving her unsure what to expect. It seemed odd to have an event of this magnitude, with bidders who would be relying on purchasing agents, and nothing detailing what exactly was up for auction.

Things made a little more sense when they were met by one of several hostesses only a few steps from the mag-lev. Dark haired and statuesque, she greeted Cris as Mr. Trace and welcomed him to the auction. Then she'd turned to Aria, smiled, and offered her another brochure.

"This is the complete catalogue for the auction. For security reasons, all materials must be returned at the end of the night. Please keep in mind that no cameras or recording equipment are permitted inside the auction area. Ms. Grove, I have a note here that you have an ocular implant, along with medical verification that it has no recording capacity. Is this correct?"

Aria nodded. She'd told this lie so many times it almost felt like the truth. "Scan functions only."

"Thank you." The hostess stepped back and gestured them onward. "Please enjoy your evening."

Cris moved toward the exhibits without another word. Aria hurried after him, playing the role she'd been assigned despite the way it chafed her to follow after Cris like a subservient minion. Next time they went undercover, she'd make sure she was the one calling the shots.

With no time to look at the new catalogue, she tucked it into her pocket to read over later. Right now, she had a job to do.

Cris kept the mission at the front of his mind as they entered the auction floor. Caspian Trace wasn't who he was. This identity was a construct, a means to an end. He'd leave it behind along with the temporary alterations to his appearance once the job was done.

He still hated it.

When it was just the two of them, it didn't bother him as much. This was different. They were swimming in dangerous waters now, surrounded by beings so much like his family he couldn't shake the feeling his mother would appear at any moment or he'd hear his father's booming laughter from some distant corner of the room. It didn't matter that they would never be caught dead in a place like this. They played their power games with a different crowd, one that pretended to be compassionate and altruistic. This group didn't bother hiding their real purpose. They were predators.

Aria's presence made it bearable. She was his anchor, a reminder that this was all an act. When they were done here, he'd go back to being who he'd chosen to be instead of a version of the man his father had wanted him to become. He'd keep telling himself that until the mission ended.

He shook his head and forced himself to focus on the here and now. The auction wasn't part of their mission, merely a way to get on board Babylon. That didn't mean it wasn't a rich source of intelligence, though. Some of the most powerful members of the underworld were here, along with their entourages and agents. They couldn't act against any of them without blowing their cover, but any information they collected would be invaluable later on.

The auction floor was massive, the dark walls creating shadowy corners and alcoves made deeper by the bright lights that highlighted each piece on display. There had to be more than a hundred guests in attendance, but they were so widely scattered that there was no sense of being crowded or a need to jostle for position. Given who some of these beings were and who they represented, it was a good choice by their hosts. Bloodshed wasn't just possible at an event like this. It was the most likely outcome.

It was easy enough to go with the flow of the crowd as they moved through the exhibits. It all felt hauntingly familiar. There was a genocidal cult leader, several warlords, heads of criminal cartels, and even a known slaver here tonight, along with dozens of agents representing those unwilling or unable to appear in person.

"Interesting company we're keeping," Aria sent through their internal link.

"Understatement of the year," he replied as he came to a stop at the first item on offer.

It was a chair that looked like it had been forged from the contents of a mad man's armory. Blades of all shapes and sizes made up most of the structure, but there were also pulse rifles, plasma grenades, and other weapons he couldn't identify since they'd been stripped and warped to fit the artist's vision. The work was entitled "seat of the warlord." It was ugly, and brutal, and entirely impractical. He did one circle around it and moved on.

A uniformed staff member approached him with a tray and offered him a glass of champagne. He took two and then turned and held them both out to Aria, who scanned them both before nodding and taking one for herself.

It had been a lot of years since he'd had to check for poison and drugs in his cocktails. It was yet another thing to add to the long list of habits he'd been happy to break after leaving home.

They moved on. This item was more interesting, or at least it would be to the man they were pretending to represent. According to their briefings, Farr preferred sculptures made of stone and polished wood. At least that's what they been able to glean from the collection of art they'd seized when he was arrested.

The sculpture was called "Breathless," and appeared to be a woman kneeling at the feet of a man, all of it carved out of flat black stone. This was exactly the sort of thing Farr preferred, so Crispin stayed to give it a closer examination, as if he were determining if this was worthy of his employer's interest.

The more he looked, the more disturbing the piece became. The woman had her hands at her throat, her mouth open, eyes wide with fear and pain. The cords of her neck stood out, as if she was struggling to breathe.

The man standing over her was in his prime, his face one of angelic beauty and utter cruelty. He looked down at the woman with disdain, and for a moment Cris couldn't understand why one figure suffered while the other didn't. Then he saw the subtle lines of an osmosis mask over the male's mouth and nose. This wasn't just dark art. It was murder made beautiful.

"*Nightmare fodder*," he said to Aria through their link.

"*I'm starting to like the chair of pointy things more and more*," she agreed.

A few seconds later, she inhaled sharply, though her expression didn't change. She still looked dispassionate and unimpressed, but he knew her well enough to see the signs. Something had her worried. Was it the sculpture or something else?

"Problem?" he asked aloud, keeping his voice soft and conversational.

"Maybe." Aria withdrew the new brochure from her pocket and read it quickly. She pursed her lips and then handed it to him, her index finger indicating the entry for the exhibit they were viewing.

The mundane descriptions of the previous brochure had been replaced by concise breakdowns and descriptions of weapons of mass destruction, illegal weapons, and a variety of other outlawed goods. "Breathless," wasn't just a statue. Apparently the winner would also receive six vials of a bio-weapon so dangerous it was banned by every government. Even the cartels wouldn't touch the stuff, but apparently there was a market for it... and they were standing in the middle of the sales floor. There was enough weaponry here to start, and possibly win, an intergalactic war.

They shared a look. None of this was connected

to their mission, but it wasn't easy to ignore something this big. Weapons like these could end civilizations and change the balance of power across the galaxy. It felt wrong to let it happen, but they couldn't do anything about it right now. Taking down VIDA had to come first.

They moved on to the next exhibit, though Cris paused long enough to drain his glass as Aria did the same. "I'll freshen your drink, sir."

"Something stronger this time, Ms. Grove." Not that even the most potent alcohol would have any effect on them. At least not for more than a minute or two, but after the revelations of the last few minutes, he wanted a drink.

"Of course."

He wandered to the nearest wall, leaned up against it, and then took the time to read over the new brochure. The seat of swords was actually a job offer, literally a request for applicants to become the heir to a warlord out in the Zerno Cluster. Several paintings had blueprints and stolen data printed on the canvas beneath the paint. It was an ingenious, low-tech way to smuggle information in a time when all digital data was subject to scrutiny.

Aria returned with two glasses of something blue and bubbling. He had no idea what it was, and he didn't bother asking. "Thank you, Ms. Grove."

"Of course, sir."

They both paused to taste the new cocktail. It

was fizzy, fruity, and had enough kick to give his medi-bots a workout. *Perfect.*

He let the first few sips settle in his stomach before pushing off the wall to make his way to the next exhibit. It was one of the few pieces that had very little information listed, even in the new brochure. Was it a purely artistic piece, or something so dangerous no one dared to spell out what it was? He hoped it was the former, but the way this night was going, it was probably the latter.

"What's this one called?" Aria asked via their link.

"Immortality Devoured."

"Not foreboding at all," even through their link, her sarcasm came through loud and clear.

At first glance, the exhibit looked quite tame and pretty compared to the others he'd seen so far. No dark colors or grim motifs here. It was a sort of sculpture, but instead of being wrought from stone or metal, its shape was formed by energy fields and gravity-plates imbedded in the bright white base. Suspended above it was a bright silver metal that flowed like molten metal, looping through the air to create the figure-eight symbol for eternity— Ouroboros—the serpent consuming itself.

It was strikingly beautiful, but something about it set off alarm bells at the back of his mind. This was bad news. He just didn't know why.

"That shouldn't be here. How did they get a sample?" Aria asked through their link.

Sample? A sample of what? He looked again. When recognition came, it was accompanied by dread and outrage. That fluid wasn't just tinted water or oil. Nor was it something as mundane as a poison or bio weapon. Judging by the volume of liquid, at least three doses of the medi-bot serum were on display, ready to be consumed. Just like the title promised, this was immortality waiting to be devoured.

Fraxx.

8

———

Someone was selling the medi-bot technology. That knowledge threw a plasma grenade into their plans. Cris was already scanning the brochure, no doubt looking for any clue as to who the seller was. Was it the Gray Men? A corporation gone rogue? Or worse, someone from the Interstellar Armed Forces who had turned traitor?

Aria ignored the surge of adrenaline that coursed through her system, mixing with the drink she just had. Her medi-bots would deal with it. All she had to do was maintain her composure and make sure that none of the tension she felt showed on her face.

Doing a casual scan of the room, she waited until her back was turned away from Crispin before she sent a message through their link. *"How do we handle this?"*

His answer was immediate. *"We don't. We can't.*

It's an unholy fraxxing mess, but we are not prepared to handle something like this. We already have one mission. If we get ourselves killed trying to take on another, then neither problem gets solved."

That was all well, true, and logical, but it didn't make her feel any better. The idea of any one of the beings in this room getting their hands on that technology made her stomach twist into knots, but right now she couldn't think of a way to stop it.

A motion at the corner of her vision caught her attention. Instinctively, she shifted position to cover Cris's back and turned to face the potential threat. It was a woman, human, dressed in a caftan of bright red with intricate yellow and orange patterns decorating the skirt and sleeves. Her skin was only a few shades lighter than Aria's, and her eyes were so dark they appeared black. Dark hair was drawn back into a twisting braid that fell almost to her waist, the tresses decorated with gemstones and bits of gold wire.

Aria recognized her instantly. This had to be the infamous Ketris. No one knew where she'd come from or how she'd gotten her start, and anyone who asked too many questions tended to vanish before they got any answers.

Ketris wasn't a criminal per se, though most of her clients were. She mediated cease-fires between cartels, acted as a third-party witness to various agreements, and arranged meetings between those in need of special services with professionals who could do the job required. Her fees were astronomical, her network envied by everyone on both sides of the law, and no one had managed to catch her breaking any law. She was one of the most dangerous beings in the galaxy, and she was headed straight for them.

Aria dropped her voice to an urgent whisper. "Incoming, sir."

Cris turned and Ketris smiled in greeting, her crimson-tinted lips curving up in a smile that was more predatory than friendly. "Caspian! How lovely to see you here."

Aria stood her ground, forcing the woman to stop and eye her with mild amusement. "Please tell your pet to put her claws away. We're old friends, after all. Have been since that night at The Rabbit."

Aria froze while her brain went into overdrive. Had this woman just used a Nova Force codeword? How was that even possible? Were their covers blown or was something else going on?

Cris nodded to the new arrival. "The Rabbit. I haven't thought about that night in years. As I recall, you were late."

Ketris's expression softened for a brief moment before she replied. "And Hatter was furious."

All three code phrases had been used. This was happening. Whatever this was...

"It's alright, Ms. Grove," Cris told her, continuing the charade.

"Yes, sir." Aria stood aside and let Ketris pass. That left her face to face with a pair of Torski females in light body armor not much different from hers. They nodded at each other and then shifted positions to form a protective ring around Crispin and Ketris.

"How are you? Still running the galaxy by proxy?" Cris asked, his tone light.

"I don't run anything," Ketris laughed and then leaned in to give Crispin an air kiss to one cheek. "What about you? I heard you're working for Tano Farr these days. You should have come to me. I would have gotten you a better deal... or a better employer."

"Next time I will."

Ketris nodded. "Do that." She lowered her voice to a coquettish whisper. "Please tell me Tano is not considering bidding on this beautiful piece. He's lived long enough already." Her tone sharpened. "In fact, some might say he's already lived too long."

"You know I can't discuss my client's plans," Cris scolded Ketris.

"And you know I have to try."

Aria could hear what they said to each other, but she was supposed to be scanning the room for threats so she couldn't watch the exchange closely. She assumed they were communicating by coded hand signals or some other subtle method.

"*Blink. Open a new channel. Victor-nine-two-alpha,*" Cris told her via their link.

She followed instructions, resisting the urge to demand more information. They were supposed to be one of the first officers to get the medi-bot treatment and the internal comm-links. So, how did this woman have one, and how the *fraxx* had she known they had them, too?

She accessed the channel, arriving in the middle of a conversation already in progress.

"*... middle of a situation you know nothing about,*" Ketris said.

"*You have your orders. We have ours,*" Cris replied.

"*I don't do orders, Lieutenant. I have operational parameters I take under advisement. Finish your mission and get the hell off this station before anyone realizes who you are or we're all* fraxxed."

"*You're here for the auction?*" Aria asked without looking in their direction.

"*The answer to that is so far above your security clearance I should kill you just for asking the question,*" Ketris replied, a hint of warning in her tone.

As they held the internal conversation, Ketris and Crispin kept up a stream of small talk about the event, the artwork, and other inane social niceties.

"*Since you're already threatening me, let me add another question. Do you know anything about the weird voice and the power fluctuation in the zoo earlier today?"* Aria asked.

"That's nothing to do with my assignment. It might have something to do with yours, but since I don't know what that is, I'm only guessing. I can tell you it started about a week ago and has increased in frequency over the last few days. No one seems to know what it is. The staff are calling it phantom. The guests are split between it being a software glitch or some kind of threat." Ketris paused and then added in a drier tone, *"This is not a group who take potential threats well. Be careful."*

"Always," Cris said before Aria could retort with something less diplomatic. *"Would you be open to keeping this channel active for twenty-four hours? Just in case that wild card proves to be something that threatens both our plans?"*

Aria expected Ketris to laugh and say no. Whoever this woman was, she clearly wasn't a team player.

Surprisingly, Ketris agreed. *"That might be wise. But only in case of emergencies. Whatever you're doing here, I don't want to know anything about it."*

"Agreed," Cris said. *"We'll stick to our mission, and you stick to yours."*

"One more question, if I may. Why risk reaching out to us at all? Doesn't that jeopardize your cover?" Aria asked.

"Everything I'm working on was put at risk the

moment the two of you unexpectedly arrived here. I'll be having a word with certain people regarding the importance of advanced notice another time. I know that if the brass thought they needed to send you in, it's a life-or-death, 'the fate of the galaxy hangs in the balance' level mission. But when is it anything less? Whatever you're here to do, get it done fast and then run like hell."

"That's our specialty," Aria said.

Ketris snorted with laughter but managed to make it seem like it was in response to something Cris had said to her. *"Good. And good luck."*

"To you too," Cris said.

Ketris moved away from the exhibit and Cris. "Enjoy the auction, Caspian. And tell your client he can't have this piece, so don't bother trying. My pockets are deeper than his."

"I'll send along the message." He winked at the other woman. "And your regards, of course."

"Of course." Ketris and her security team departed. Aria held position long enough to see the woman making straight for another small group clustered around an obelisk of red stone. She was still a meter away when she raised a hand in greeting. "Tisk! I didn't expect to see you here."

Cris strode past Aria. "With me. I need to talk to my employer."

"Yes, sir."

She followed him to one of the balconies that

ringed the massive lobby. It offered privacy and a change of scenery, both of which were welcome. Cris chose one directly above the waterfall. They were close enough to it to feel the mist in the air, and the noise drowned out anything they said.

She claimed a spot on the railing, far enough away to give her "boss" some privacy while still sticking close enough to do her job.

"*That was unexpected,*" she said through their link.

Cris stared down at the looping course of the gravity-defying river. "*Very. But it means we can focus on our mission and leave the auction to Ketris... or whatever her name really is. I had no idea Nova Force had agents doing that kind of deep cover work.*"

"*I'm not sure she's an agent,*" Aria said.

"*Neither am I. But she is an asset, and a very well-informed one. She had our cover details and knew we had implants. We didn't even know she was here.*"

"*Yeah. And here I thought we were somewhere near the top of the IAF food chain, at least when it came to this sort of thing. I don't know if I'm relieved or disappointed to discover that's not the case.*" Aria glanced down at the drink in her hand. She hadn't touched it since Ketris had made herself known. As much as she'd enjoyed the first few sips, she'd be sticking to water for the rest of the night.

"*Me either,*" Cris admitted.

"*You good on your own for a few minutes? I need a fresh drink and a chance to scan a few more faces for review later.*"

"*I'll be fine. I'm not really in need of a bodyguard... or a babysitter.*"

"*Says the man I saved from a slavering six-legged beastie just a few hours ago.*"

Instead of replying, Cris turned to her, winked slightly and held out his empty glass, shaking it so the remaining ice cubes rattled.

"Another of the same, sir?" she asked while sending another message via their link. "*Asshole.*"

"Just my usual," he said aloud and added. "*I'm in character.*"

"Yes, sir. Coming up." And between them she sent, "*Your character is an asshole.*"

"*I'm aware of that. But since he's supposed to be that way, and he employs your character... off you go to fetch me a drink.*"

Aria took the glass from her "boss" and left the balcony. "*Try not to get into trouble while I'm gone.*"

"*I'll manage.*"

She knew he would. Cris was one of the most capable men she'd ever known. *Would* ever know. Every guy she'd flirted with since had failed to measure up... which was why she'd never gotten serious with anyone else.

Well, hell. She picked a fine time to have a romantic revelation about her coworker. Part of an old conversation she'd had with Nyx came back to haunt her. "For someone with enhanced vision, you don't see things as well as you should."

Nyx had been right back then, but there'd been more to her words than just a warning that Aria was misinterpreting Cris's behavior. It was bigger than that.

Fraxx.

If they survived the next few days, she'd have to buy the cyborg a drink... and maybe share some of that insanely good chocolate.

As disturbing as it was to discover they weren't the only operatives on the station, Crispin had to admit he was relieved to know that the auction and all it entailed was officially someone else's problem. It was the one bit of good news in what had been a day full of challenges. They still needed to figure out a way to get into VIDA's vault without being caught. Wandering through a botanical garden open day and night would have been simple enough. Crossing an exposed bridge in a well-monitored area that was closed each night would require a little more finesse. Then, they had to work out how to get off the station without being killed... or worse.

With most of the guests here to attend the auction, the easiest option was to hit the vault once the bidding started. That meant missing the event, though. If they didn't show, would it be noticed? And how the *fraxx* did they get around the tracking bands they both wore?

Once they were back in their suite, they'd have to make plans. Aria would have something in mind already. She always did. He had a few ideas, too. Between them, they'd find a way to get this done—preferably one that allowed them both to walk out of here with their heads still attached.

While he thought, he spoke into his comms, making it look like he was making a report subvocally. It was all a ruse, of course. All the connections had been made, but no one was on the receiving end. They had no way to know if anyone was watching communication traffic, but he suspected if the station itself wasn't, some of the other guests would be.

Footsteps sounded behind him and he turned, expecting to see Aria with their drinks. He opened his mouth to greet her, only to have his world explode with bright light and pain as something slammed into his jaw.

"You son of a star-beast. I knew it was you!"

Years of combat training kicked in as Crispin instinctively dropped into a fighting crouch and stepped away from the railing at his back before his attacker found a way to pin him against it. By the time his scrambled senses could work out what was going on, he'd already blocked another sloppy punch.

Then he got a good look at his assailant and silently cursed the universe's timing. What was Phillip doing *here*, of all places? He blocked another blow and decided that now was not the time to ponder the odds against this happening. First he needed to deal with Phillip *fraxxing* Farthington before the damned fool blew his cover.

"I have no idea who you think I am, but I've never met you before in my life." At least Phil hadn't changed much. He was a big man, built on a scale that would impress a Torski, but apparently he still drank too much and couldn't throw a decent punch.

"Crispy! I told you if I ever saw you again, you'd regret it!"

"Hey, Blink. Little help here."

"I left you alone for two minutes... what could you possibly have... holy fraxx, *I see the problem. On my way."*

He sidestepped a clumsy kick and kept moving. Phil followed him, his movements slowed by booze or whatever pharma he'd consumed tonight. Picking a fight like this was a bad idea in most places he could think of. Here? It was almost suicidal.

"Throw one more punch and this is going to get ugly. For the last time, I'm not this Crispy guy. My name's Trace."

"Bullshit! I know it's you!"

Cris sighed and made a show of looking regretful. It would help sell his case when station security reviewed the footage later. He took one more step, and Phil followed him, oblivious to the fact he was now the one standing with his back to the railing... and a long fall to the lobby floor below.

"You are messing with the wrong guy. Last warning."

Phillip scoffed. "You don't scare me, little man. You were always better with your mouth than your hands."

Little man? Cris knew he couldn't respond, but part of him wanted to quit pretending and defend his honor. His hands were just as talented as his mouth, thank you very much, and nothing about him was even close to little.

It was probably a good thing Aria showed up at that moment.

Instead of running straight to the balcony he was on, she dashed to the one on his right.

She barely slowed down as she pivoted and then sped up again before running straight toward them... and then she launched herself into the air.

Knowing she had a cybernetic leg was one thing. Seeing her actually use it was something else again.

She soared over the railing, crossing the gap between the balconies with ease. She landed gracefully and lunged at Phillip with her stun baton, slamming it into the big man's side.

The baton released its charge, but instead of dropping Phillip to the floor in a twitching heap, it only seemed to infuriate him. He roared and turned toward Aria, catching her with a backhanded swing she had no chance to block as she continued to try and stun him.

The blow was hard enough to make Aria stagger. She retreated, shaking her head to clear it as she frantically adjusted the baton's settings.

"I warned you," Cris said, his voice pure ice and venom now. Sucker punching him was bad enough, but now that Phil had laid hands on Aria, all bets were off.

Phillip took the bait, looking away from Aria to glare at Cris again. That gave Aria the second she needed, and she darted forward again. This time, she caught him in the stomach, driving the head of the weapon deep.

Phil's entire body tensed and bowed as the energy blast locked his muscles. He'd be down and out in seconds, but that wasn't going to be enough. Not for the man Cris was pretending to be.

Cris charged in, throwing a frontal kick that caught Phil high on his chest. Muscles still frozen, Phil could do nothing to stop what happened next. His bulky body toppled backward, the momentum enough to make him crash into the railing. If he'd been a shorter man, that would have been the end of it, but Phillip was so tall that he continued falling, toppling over the railing and vanishing from view.

A chorus of startled screams rose up from the lobby below.

Aria stared at the empty space where Phil had stood a moment earlier. "Did you just..."

Cris shrugged as if it was of no concern if his attacker lived or died. "The ugly bastard attacked me. I warned him. Twice. What happened to him was his own fault."

"You're bleeding, sir. Shall I call for a medic?"

"I'm sure one will be arriving shortly." He dusted off his clothes, straightening the fabric and putting himself back in order. "Along with a number of security guards with questions."

"Yes, sir." She wandered over to the railing and looked down. Then she turned and smiled at him. "You might enjoy seeing this, sir."

He could hear the security team sprinting toward them, but he ignored it and went to join Aria at the railing. A very wet and groggy Phillip floated along a portion of the river several stories above the lobby floor. He was awake enough to keep his head above the water but didn't appear to be willing or able to try and do more than that.

Security arrived while he was still at the railing, watching Phillip float along as more staff members scrambled to reach him before the river brought him to the top of the waterfall.

"Sir, ma'am, please place your hands in the air and turn around slowly." The request was almost polite. Aria glanced over at him, a smile dancing on her lips. "This day just keeps getting better."

They both raised their hands and turned toward the waiting security force. "*And it's not over yet.*" He sent to her via their feed.

"What happened here?" the same Torski security officer they'd seen upon arrival demanded.

Cris squared his shoulders and gave the male a cool look. "I have no idea. That man attacked me for no reason. Punched me before we'd even said a word to each other. He wasn't making much sense. He accused me of being someone called Crispy. He's deranged and dangerous. If he's not off this station within the hour, there will be consequences. I want him gone. If I see that deranged lunatic again, I will do more than just give him an impromptu swimming lesson. Are we clear?"

Synda and Ramon arrived, pushing their way through the pack of security. Several medics followed close behind. Synda rushed toward him, her pretty face twisted with concern and more than a little trepidation. "Mr. Trace! Are you alright? What do you need? What can I do for you?"

Aria reacted so quickly he barely saw her move. One moment she was a few steps away, and the next she was standing in front of him, one hand outstretched. "You don't go near him. No one does.

Taking care of Mr. Trace's *needs* is my job, not yours."

The Pheran blinked. Everyone got quiet, and Cris had to fight like hell not to break into a victory dance.

Aria had just staked a claim on him. All it had taken to make that happen was a near-death experience, an unexpected assault, and the attention of an attractive female willing to do anything he asked of her. Honestly, he'd thought it would be harder...

Now, he needed to get her alone before she changed her mind.

9

———

One thing Aria could say about the station security, they were efficient. They were also surprisingly polite. That probably had something to do with the fact that everyone security interacted with was rich enough to buy and sell planets. That had to be an incentive to be nice or risk losing your job... or worse.

She and Cris were escorted to a lounge area as comfortable and luxurious as the rest of this orbiting palace. Once they were seated, their liaisons Ramon and Synda insisted on delaying the process until they confirmed that both their guests were comfortable. They even offered to fetch food and drinks. Amused, Aria requested a cup of black tea and cookies. Cris requested an ice water. Security waited impassively until the liaisons left to fulfill their orders before proceeding. Clearly this was something they were used to, and it spoke volumes about how constrained they had to be when dealing with beings as dangerous and powerful as the station's guests.

After some preliminary questions establishing their identities, their reasons for being on board the station, and other basic details, she and Cris were escorted to separate rooms for questioning. Interestingly, these rooms had windows that allowed them to see each other. It was a questionable practice, but again, the rules here were different. As interrogations went, it was the nicest she had ever been to. The rooms were well-appointed, the chairs exceedingly comfortable, and the tea Ramon brought her was perfectly brewed.

The questions were simple and straightforward. No one tried to twist her words. There were no leading questions or head games. They asked for her version of events, clarified a few details and then moved on. They wanted to know if her employer had any violent tendencies she was aware of. They also inquired as to why a man with his obvious combat skills felt the need to hire a bodyguard.

It was a fair question, one she was prepared for. "I imagine I was hired to ensure he didn't have to get his hands dirty. Mr. Trace does not enjoy blood, sweat, or public confrontation."

They seemed to accept this. In fact, they accepted everything she said without question or comment. It probably helped that the entire incident had been captured on multiple security cameras, and all of them would confirm what she told them.

Once the interview wound down, she asked a question of her own. "Is the male who attacked my client off the station, or should I be prepared to see him again?"

The human woman asking most of the questions answered her. "For the time being, he is still on the station. His guest status has been revoked and his sponsor was informed of the incident."

"And that means?" Aria asked.

The woman smiled for the first time. It wasn't a pleasant expression. "Mr. Farthington will be gone before you and your client are finished here. His sponsor was given the choice to either remove him from his entourage or depart at the same time he does. You will not see the suspect again."

Aria nodded crisply. "That would be for the best. Mr. Trace does not make threats. If he sees that man again, he *will* kill him." She shrugged slightly and turned her hands palm up. "Or ask me to do it."

No one looked surprised at her admission. In fact, they looked as if they were expecting it. A chill chased down her spine. It was a grim reminder that they were out of their element here. The laws and rules they were accustomed to didn't apply.

"I know we've already covered this," someone else said. "But are you sure your client had no previous encounters with the suspect? He is quite adamant he knows Mr. Trace as someone called Crispin Caldwell."

The well-rehearsed lie flowed easily off her tongue. "I haven't worked with him for all that long, but I did my own research before I signed on with him. Mr. Trace is exactly who he claims to be. Whoever this Coldwell person is, it's not my client."

"Caldwell," the same man corrected her, but his tone was casual with no rancor or even concern.

"Right. Sorry, it's been a long day." Aria pinched the bridge of her nose as if warding off a headache. She took a moment to sip her tea before returning to the topic. "I can tell you that in the time I have known Mr. Trace, he has never met with that man or spoken of him. I haven't seen so much as an image of him. Not until he attacked my client."

This time the lead officer spoke. "Do you believe Mr. Trace intended for his attacker to be caught by the gravitational forces manipulating the river?"

This was a tricky question, but one she'd already worked out how to answer with outright lying. "If my client had wanted that man dead, he would no longer be breathing."

She knew Cris had hoped Phillip would fall into the water. Not only because it would likely keep him alive, but because the dip would wash away any possible genetic material that might have been on the man's clothing after their little dustup. While Dr. Li had treated both their outer layers of skin to alter any

DNA that might be shed, it wasn't one-hundred-percent effective. It would be easier and safer if there was simply no evidence to find.

Her interview ended a few minutes later. She still had half a cup of tea to drink and two more cookies to eat, so she took them with her when she was escorted back to the main lounge. She was still finishing her snack when Cris appeared, looking calm, relaxed, and heart-achingly attractive. He might be walking out of a business meeting instead of an interrogation. He claimed a seat across from her and they sat in comfortable silence for a few minutes while she finished off the last of her cookies. She was going to have to put in an order to room service for more. They were damn good.

She ignored Synda as the little Pheran joined Ramon in the far corner of the room. She gave Aria a wary glance before turning to talk to her counterpart. *Good.* She'd gotten the message. The last thing this evening needed was a dose of their liaisons' desire-enhancing pheromones. At least, that was the story she was telling herself. It was easier than admitting she was jealous, though she was painfully aware of how foolish she was acting. Of all the times to lay claim to Cris, she'd chosen now. It was stupid and reckless, but she couldn't bring herself to regret it. It felt right, even if the timing was all wrong.

As she set her teacup back in its saucer, Crispin cleared his throat. "I believe it's time for me to retire,

Miss Grove." Then he glanced around the room at the various security guards still lingering. "Unless there's something else you need me for?"

One of them checked a comm unit, his eyes moving as he read the screen. Then he looked up and nodded to Cris. "You and your employee can leave now, Mr. Trace. I hope you have a pleasant evening."

Synda and Ramon stopped talking. The liaisons both moved at the same time, headed straight for them. Cris ignored them completely, but Aria made a sharp gesture that made it clear their services would not be needed. Both of them stopped, and for a moment, she thought she saw a look of relief on Ramon's face. *Interesting.*

Then she answered Cris. "As you say, sir."

She couldn't wait to get out of here. The two of them needed to get back to their suite. It was the one place they could talk without being observed or overheard. She had questions about what had really happened, and they still needed to come up with a plan to complete their mission. Something told her they were running out of time to get this done and get the hell off Babylon Station before anything else went wrong.

They had to check the map on their wristbands to find their way back to their suite. "*This would have*

been easier if we had a guide. Like, oh, say the two beings whose job it is to help us while we're on the station," Cris quipped through their link as they stopped to get their bearings again.

"Are you questioning my navigation skills?" she retorted.

"I'm pretty sure we've already passed that painting once before, so... maybe?" Cris said.

"I don't need your pretty little Pheran to find our room. And that is not the same painting. The artwork is color-coded to the sections. The last time we saw that print, it was in done in aqua-blue. In our section everything is green."

"There's a difference?" he asked, his confusion clear even over the link.

She wasn't sure how the males of her species had survived this long given how little attention they paid to details. "This way, sir," she said out loud and pointed down the hallway to their suite.

Cris shot her a wry smile. "Thank you, Ms. Grove."

They kept up the internal banter until they were safely back inside their suite. Neither of them said anything until she completed a sweep of the entire place and confirmed everything was secure.

"Clear," she said and then turned to look at Cris. "Now, what the *fraxx* was that about?"

Cris ran a hand lightly over his jaw. He'd asked for a cloth to clean up the blood from his split lip but had declined any other treatment. No sense letting a medic get close enough to see he how fast he was healing. "That was Phil. I guess he's still mad I slept with his sister."

"He got himself tossed off the station because you banged his sister? That seems a bit extreme."

Cris shot her a wicked, lopsided grin. "I suspect it has more to do with the fact I was dating him at the time."

"Oh holy *fraxx*. That was *the* Phil? The one who wrecked his hover-bike trying to chase you down the night he caught you with his sister?" She shook her head in disbelief. "How did he recognize you? It's been years!"

"I have no idea. But the purpose of these alterations was to fool facial recognition scans, not living beings. I can't even calculate the odds that someone I knew from my old life would be here. His parents would disown him if they knew."

"If he's here, the disowning has likely already happened. You and your sister are the only elite types I've ever met who walked away from that life and never looked back. Most can't do it. Like your Phil. He's not here on his own. He was just part of someone else's entourage. Another lackey clinging to the trappings of wealth." Now that she'd been to Babylon and gotten a small taste of what it was like to live that way, she finally understood the attraction. It wasn't just the luxury of it all. It was the sense of importance. Everything here, from the gift bags to the beings personally assigned to ensure the guests' complete satisfaction, created an environment where the guests were truly the center of the universe. Even she was treated this way, and her role as bodyguard meant she was barely a step above the station's staff.

"He was never very bright. He'd do anything to maintain the illusion of wealth and influence while I can't wait to get the hell out of here and away from all this." He gestured around them.

"Caspian Trace isn't who you are." She cocked her head and deliberately changed the subject. "Though I kind of like the new hair. The rest can go, though."

"I'm looking forward to seeing your eyes their usual color, too. Dark brown and full of sass." He grinned. "Sassy and silver isn't the same."

"I still don't recognize myself in the mirror. I can't believe Phillip recognized you."

Cris grimaced and raked a hand through his hair. "I showed Dr. Li pictures of what I used to look like back when I was part of this world. The fairer hair and darker skin tone are similar to that time period. I just didn't expect to see anyone I knew."

"Yeah, about that." She cocked her head to one side. "What are the chances of us running into any more of your ex-lovers before this mission is over?"

His eyes crinkled in the corners and she prepared for a glib answer, but then his expression turned serious. "Phil was a long time ago. I was young and stupid, but even so, I knew better than to cause too much scandal for my father."

She should have stopped there, but her next question slipped out before her filters activated. "Anyone more recent I need to know about? For the mission, that is."

He stared at her in silence for several seconds, long enough she was about to retract the question and flee to her room in mortification. She shouldn't have asked that. It was out of line, personal, and utterly unprofessional, especially considering she was a trained interrogator.

"I shouldn't have—"

He surprised her, walking right up to her and catching her chin in one gentle hand. "There's been no one since you, Ri."

They were standing on ice so thin she could almost hear it cracking. This time, she let it break. "I told you to move on. Why didn't you?"

"Because there wasn't anyone else I wanted to move on with." Cris locked gazes with her, and she saw the truth shining in his eyes.

He'd never given up on her.

"I'm a *fraxxing* idiot," she murmured, looping one arm around his waist and stepping in closer.

"Yeah, you are. But so am I. I should have done this years ago."

Then he kissed her. It was a hard, hungry kiss,

full of passion and a hint of dominance she didn't remember from the last time they'd done this. He'd been a stranger then, flirtatious and fun. His tongue slid along the seam of her lips. She knew what he wanted. In. Into her mouth. Into her body, and into her life.

She opened herself to him, and with one kiss, all the years of excuses and denial melted away, leaving her with one searing truth. She wanted him. She always had... and she always would.

Crispin wanted to devour her. To tear off her clothes and lose himself in the beauty of her body until everything else disappeared. But he waited instead, giving her one last chance to stop him, to retreat behind the walls she'd put between them. Barriers he'd done his best to respect... until now.

Aria rose on her toes to kiss him back, her lips parting as a soft moan of need rose from her throat.

Yes.

He slid his fingers over her hair to cup the back of her head, pulling her in close as he slanted his lips over hers.

His other hand slid down her back until he was palming the soft curve of her ass. *Fraxx*, he had forgotten how good she felt.

She softened in his arms, rubbing herself against

him in ways that threatened his sanity. She smelled like the expensive cleansers the showers were stocked with, something clean and citrusy that reminded him of hot summer days and cold lemonade.

Warm hands stroked down his back, moving over the soft silk of his shirt until she reached his waist. She untucked his shirt and reached beneath, giving him the skin-to-skin contact they both craved.

She moaned, the soft sound flowing through him like the most perfect note in the galaxy. He'd waited so long to hear it again.

"I know you like it slow, Ri. But I can't. Not this time."

"This time I don't want slow. I just want you." She tipped her head back to look at him, her fingers curving just enough that her nails bit into his flesh. "Quick. Before I remember all the reasons I was sure this was a bad idea."

Her words were light and teasing, but that didn't matter. He wouldn't let her change her mind. Not this time. He tightened his hold on her, pulling her in hard against his body as he held her gaze. "No."

Her mouth tightened, but at the same time a flash of fire kindled in her eyes. "No?"

"We did things your way for the last three years." He rocked his hips, pressing the hard ridge of his cock against her soft body. "Now we're going to do things *my* way."

"And what's your way?" A hint of challenge crept into her words, and he reveled in it.

"Hard, fast, and as often as possible." He almost added, "and for the rest of my life," but managed to stop himself. That was a conversation for another time. He didn't want to talk right now. He wanted to show her where she belonged, and to whom. He cupped her face in both hands and then leaned down to kiss her again. "I've missed you."

The light in her eyes shone brighter as she raised one hand to cover his. "Stars help me, I've missed you, too."

He walked her backward, not stopping until she reached the nearest wall. It happened to be the one with viewports showing the stars outside.

"Computer, activate stargazer mode for this suite."

After a soft chime of acknowledgment, the lights dimmed and the wall behind Aria vanished.

"What's stargazer... oh!" Aria glanced over her shoulder and saw for herself. "Nice! How did you know the command for that?"

"I read the welcome brochure while you were still processing the obscene amount of wealth crammed into the bag." He realized his mistake the moment the words left his mouth, so he followed up with a soul-searing kiss that stopped her from thinking about the gift bags or anything else. Now was no time for thinking.

When he finally released her from the kiss, she laughed and slapped him lightly on the chest. "I don't remember you being this pushy last time."

"Last time we were almost strangers. This time, I know what I want. You. Naked. Now."

Heat made her eyes gleam like molten silver as she reached up to a tab near her throat. He hadn't noticed it before, but now all his attention was locked onto it as she tugged it slowly downward.

When she reached the level of her breast bone, he stepped back to get a better view. With just enough light to let him see as she undressed, she peeled off the body suit in slow, languid motions that left him dazed and on edge at the same time. She looked like a goddess out of humanity's distant past, all dark skin and glimmers of gold as she revealed herself to him against the backdrop of stars.

He stripped off his clothes without taking his eyes off her, ignoring the slight tremble in his fingers as he pulled them off and dropped them in a pile at his feet.

"Damn, Trip. Did you lift the weights or eat them?" Aria asked. Her seductive striptease hit a snag when the bodysuit hit the tops of her boots, which she'd forgotten to take off first.

Cris flexed everything he could and grinned at her, suddenly feeling like a young man with his first crush. "You like?"

"I like." She crooked a finger at him. "So get over

here and let me do a hands-on inspection."

"Yes, ma'am." He closed the short distance between them, placing a hand on each side of her head to box her in before moving in for a kiss. He'd never get enough of her—not her taste, or her body, or the way her smile warmed even the darkest corners of his soul.

Their tongues danced, mouths open and the sounds of need rising from their throats to blend together as she stroked her hands over his body. Her touch was gentle, but her fingers were callused and strong. Her strength was one of the things he'd always been drawn to, even though he suspected her need to be strong was the real reason she'd insisted they couldn't be more than friends.

Each kiss was hotter than the last, his cock pressed up against the bare curve of her belly as her fingers left tiny trails of fire across his skin. When he couldn't hold back any longer, he dropped to his knees at her feet and helped her with her boots, tossing them aside with no care where they landed. Then he removed her body suit with impatient tugs.

He had one leg free when he let himself look up at her and his breath locked in his lungs for several seconds before he managed to speak again. "You've been naked all night?"

"I wasn't naked. I was commando. When wearing something that tight, panty lines are to be avoided."

"I... you... naked." His thoughts came out like a garbled radio message, broken and incoherent.

"I won't be naked until you finish undressing me." Her expression altered, becoming that of a regal queen looking down at her servant as she lifted her leg and placed her bare foot on his thigh. "You may continue."

He slid the fabric over her calf and foot before casting it aside. Then he surged forward, lifting her leg up over his shoulder with his other hand on her waist to steady her.

She made a little sound of surprise, but then her hands were in his hair, guiding him toward where they both needed him to be. The soft skin of her inner thighs caressed his cheeks as he got his first taste of her, the lips of her pussy already wet and swollen with arousal. Now she had her balance, he let go of her waist and let his hand drift down her hip to her thigh before bringing it to the apex of her thighs. He held still for a moment, his tongue pressed against her clit.

He didn't move until she shivered and arched her hips away from the wall, her hands pulling his head in closer. "More."

He laughed as he shifted his hand, using his fingers to caress and fuck her as his tongue continued to focus on her clit.

"*Fraxxing* hell. Yes!" she cried out, one hand slamming against the wall as she rode his mouth, taking what she needed. His cock ached with the need to be inside her, but they weren't there... yet. He needed to watch her come apart first and feel her clamp around his fingers as her cream flowed over his lips and tongue.

It didn't take long to achieve his goal. The heat between them was almost enough to make the air shimmer as they gave in to needs that had only grown in the years they'd been apart. Her fingers tightened on his scalp, nails pricking at his skin as she uttered a wild cry and came. He didn't stop, pushing her farther into her release and drawing out every second of pleasure as she gasped and shuddered. Every sound she uttered made him harder, and the taste of her was almost enough to break his control.

When her cries had quieted, he raised his head, wiping his mouth with the back of one hand as he stared up at the beauty before him. She was still a goddess but momentarily sated, her breath coming in soft pants.

"Did I mention that I've missed you?" she murmured with a smile.

"You might have, but I like hearing it." He stood and pulled her back into his arms for another kiss. He wanted her to taste herself on him and remember that he was the one who turned her world upside down with pleasure. Him. No one else. She might not realize it yet, but she belonged to him, and he wasn't letting her go. Not this time.

When he broke their kiss, she made a soft noise of protest in the back of her throat and tried to follow him, wanting more.

He gave it to her.

He caught her hips in his hands and then slid them down until he was cupping her ass. "Up."

Her brows rose at the command in his tone, but she followed his instructions. She hopped up, using the strength in her cybernetic leg to push up as he lifted her. Within seconds she was in his arms, legs wrapped around his waist, her arms draped over his shoulders.

"You sure you can..." she started to ask, but he cut her off with a hard kiss before answering.

"Am I sure I can fuck you up against this wall until you scream my name again? Yes, yes I am. Allow me to demonstrate."

He was hard enough he could have punched through the hull of a battle cruiser, the tip sliding along the slick seam of her pussy and teasing them both.

"Haven't we wasted enough time already?" Aria asked, her voice thick with need as she wriggled her hips.

"*We* didn't waste that time. As I recall, you were the one who ended things, not me."

She huffed in frustration and more than a little laughter. "You're bringing this up now?"

He shifted his stance, pushing his cock into

position but holding himself at her entrance by sheer force of will. "This time, we're not going to end. Not until the last stars fade and the universe falls into darkness. I'm not letting you go again, Aria."

It was too soon. He knew that, but the words spilled out before he could stop himself. He needed her to hear him, to understand what this moment meant.

Her silver eyes gleamed as she stared back at him. The silence stretched out for what felt like an eternity, though it couldn't have been more than a few seconds. Then, she laughed, soft and low, and said, "I'm starting to like this new, pushy version of you."

"Good, because he's not going anywhere." With that, he thrust into her, burying himself to the hilt inside the welcoming heat of her body.

Her legs tightened around him as he brought his mouth crashing down on hers, the two of them coming together in a blaze of need and fire. She moaned his name, the sound buzzing against his lips as they kissed. They moved at the same moment, quickly finding the rhythm that worked best for them. Her inner walls pulsed around his cock each time he withdrew, stroking his length and bringing him to the edge of his control faster than he'd ever experienced before.

She tore her lips from his and then dropped her

head to bury her face in the crook of his neck. *Fraxx.* She remembered.

She nipped the side of his neck sharply, the pain of it a perfect contrast to the pleasure coursing through him. His cock jerked and his balls tightened, his entire body going rigid for a moment as he fought to stay in control.

With a wicked laugh, she did it again, this time with an opened-mouthed bite that ended with a swipe of her tongue over the spot.

His control shattered.

He threw back his head and cursed as he slammed into her, fucking her hard and fast as his orgasm tore through him. Her body clamped down around his, milking his cock. He lifted her slightly, changing the angle just enough to increase the contact between his cock and her clit each time he withdrew. She clawed at his shoulders, her voice rising to a breathless cry as her release started. He felt every pulse and quiver as he emptied himself inside her.

When they were both spent, he lowered them both to the floor with him on the bottom and her resting on top of him, her head on his chest.

"That was..." he didn't know how to end the sentence so he trailed off.

"Yeah, it was. Wanna do it again?" she asked, looking up at him with a wicked little smile.

"*Fraxx*, yes." An idea dawned, along with the

10

Thanks to her medi-bots, Aria didn't need much sleep. But after the night she'd just shared with Cris, she had needed a few hours of rest. It had never occurred to her that their nanotech-enhanced endurance would affect her sex-life. But hell's bells and gravity wells, it was a definite improvement.

Or maybe it was because she was with Cris again...

She woke up slowly, not ready to face the day just yet. Cris was snuggled up behind her, his presence making her feel safe and warm in a way she rarely experienced.

It had been years since she'd spent all night in her lover's bed. She was more the kind to take what she needed and then slip away long before her partner woke up.

Waking up like this was nice. Though if she was

being honest with herself, nice was a mild word for it —a safe word that stayed far away from the rising storm of questions and feelings she wasn't ready to deal with. Was this what she wanted? Was *Cris* who she wanted to be with?

Nope. She wasn't doing this right now. Mission first. Madness later.

Pushing all that aside, she allowed herself to be distracted by Cris, who was sliding a gentle hand up and down her thigh. What he was doing was more tempting than dwelling on the future. At least it was until she realized what he was doing wasn't so much a seduction as an examination.

She stiffened as his fingertips brushed over the almost imperceptible scars that marked the attachment points between her original body and her replacement leg. It made her feel vulnerable and exposed, and she had to remind herself that this was Cris, who knew all her secrets and flaws and wanted her anyway.

She opened her eyes and spoke but didn't turn to look at him. "Good morning. You know, if you were curious, you could've just asked. I mean, it's not like you haven't seen my scans. And you were in the med-bay when we did the alterations to my appearance."

Cris's hand froze and then he uttered a soft, somewhat guilty sigh. "It's not that. I was just... I mean, does it hurt? Ever?"

So that was it. "No. Honestly, most of the time I don't notice the difference. If anything, this one aches less." She rolled over so she could see him and give him a little smile. "This one has a lot less wear and tear."

He didn't say anything. He just looked at her, his hand still on her leg and his thumb moving in tiny circles over her skin.

She realized he was waiting for her to say more. This wasn't something she liked to talk about. Not even with the cyborgs who had helped her come to terms with her new reality. "I would notice phantom pains at first. Nerve endings all confused by the trauma and not sure what sensations to believe." She waved down at her leg. "But it really doesn't bother me anymore. I mean it doesn't hurt. It still bothers me sometimes. I'm a lot less human than I used to be."

He scowled. "You're one of the most human people I have ever met. It doesn't matter what parts of you are original and what are upgrades. It doesn't even matter what species you are. You're incredible, Ri. Please don't ever forget that."

His scowl deepened. She saw worry there, and fear, and guilt. "I'm glad it doesn't hurt you anymore."

Aria had a moment of understanding. "Dammit, Trip, I thought we were past this. Are you still feeling guilty? Don't be an idiot. What you did... I can't imagine how hard it would have been to do that. But you did it, and it's the only reason I didn't die. If you hadn't cut off what was left of my leg..." She shook her head, not able to continue. "I'm sorry you had to do that. If I had been faster, then maybe—"

He hauled her into his arms and kissed her with a desperate hunger that she felt all the way down to her soul. "Don't you dare blame yourself. Nyx hauled me out of there first, and I let her. I shouldn't have. I should have made her take you. Then you wouldn't have gotten hurt."

"And what would have happened then? You would have been caught in the explosion instead of me. You're our medic. None of us have your skills. Even the automated med-system couldn't have treated that kind of trauma as well as you did."

He shook his head, his voice thick with guilt as he said, "It should have been me."

Aria laughed suddenly as the insanity of their situation dawned. They were both being far too hard on themselves. "We can't go on blaming ourselves for what happened. Can we? If we do, it's going to make for a very long lifetime."

"Especially since we both have medi-bots now." He grinned at her. "I don't suppose you'd consider..."

The power fluctuated, and they heard that demented cackling, though she had no idea where the *fraxx* it was coming from.

What little ambient light had been in the room vanished, plunging them into darkness so absolute she couldn't see her hand in front of her face even with her dark light filter in her cybernetic eye. The sense of disorientation only got worse as the gravity misbehaved again. Caught in total darkness, the loss of gravity stripped away all sense of direction. Her mind screamed as she scrambled to cope with the almost total lack of sensory input.

Cris wrapped his arms around her, and she did the same, the two of them holding tightly to the only solid thing in their current existence—each other.

"For the love of gravity, again?" Cris groaned. He was barely audible above the demented laughter that filled the air.

"I'm really starting to hate this *fraxxing* place," Aria muttered.

Before either of them could get a hold of anything else, the gravity reactivated. That would have been fine, but it had also reoriented itself. Instead of settling back onto the comfortable mattress, they "fell" toward their new down. She had no idea if it was a wall or the ceiling that they slammed into, though she really hoped it was a wall or the next time gravity reset, it was going to hurt.

They both hit with a thump hard enough to drive the breath from their lungs and she cracked her head against the surface hard enough the darkness was momentarily filled with stars. The power returned and all the lights came on, nearly blinding her, but her cybernetic eye adjusted quickly, allowing her to make out where she was—halfway up the wall on her side of the bed.

The static-filled laughter shifted to gabbled words that she struggled to understand. "Traitorous bitch... They're coming now... You'll be sorry..."

"What the *fraxx* is that thing?" Cris snarled in frustration. Then, the gravity changed again, and they fell to the floor. Crispin managed to get between her and the impact, though slamming into his hard muscular body wasn't much better than slamming into the floor.

Once she had enough breath in her lungs to speak, she said, "This is getting seriously weird."

"Which part?" Cris asked dryly.

"Pretty much all of it."

She caught the twitch of his brows and knew right away what he was thinking. "No. Not that bit. I have a lot of words to describe last night, but weird is not one of them."

"Good. I liked that bit too and plan on doing it again just as soon as we're clear of this place."

As good as last night had been, she wasn't ready to commit to a repeat performance. At least, not just yet. "Hold that thought until after the mission." She leaned down to kiss him softly, letting her lips linger against his.

He caught the back of her head in his hand,

pulling her in close and kissing her with a ferocity that made her blood sing and the room spin.

When he finally released her, she didn't move right away. She gave herself a moment to indulge in the raw attraction she was feeling for him. It had never gone away, and now that she'd acknowledged it, she wasn't sure she'd ever be able to deny her feelings again. Even more terrifying... she didn't want to do that.

The cocky bastard knew it, too, because he tucked both hands under his head, grinned at her, and then winked. "Once this mission ends, you have five minutes. Consider yourself warned."

She hid the effect of his words with a loud snort of laughter and pushed herself off him, managing to give his chest a playful slap in the process. It was like slapping hull plating. "I'll take that under advisement. Right now, we have things to do."

"I don't do break and enters before breakfast."

She nodded and got to her feet, grateful for her nanotech. It was already erasing what few aches and pains she had after this morning's gravitational mishaps... and last night's wild indulgence. "Breakfast sounds good. I'll put in our orders with the food dispenser and then hit the shower. We can finalize our plans over food." She paused and then added. "Do you think that... whatever the hell it is will be a problem? The last thing we need is a gravity failure when we're standing over a tank full of carnivorous fish."

Cris grimaced. "I know, but we have no idea what it is or why it's happening. I think we're just going to have to assume this entire mission was sponsored by Murphy and his laws."

"Truth. It's damned creepy, though. Like this place has its own demented poltergeist roaming around, cackling randomly and causing chaos." She glanced at Cris, who had gotten up and was now pacing around the bedroom stark naked. "And I still think I've heard that voice before somewhere. I can't place it, though. One thing for sure, whoever or whatever it is, it's not sane. Not even close."

"Let's hope Magi dug up something useful. I'm going to check the data cache we set up and see if we've heard anything from the team. Oh, and if you want a real treat, see if they've got eggs benedict on the menu. I'll take mine with a double side of real bacon."

"What the hell is eggs benedict?" she asked.

"I'm pretty sure it's the best breakfast in this or any other galaxy. Better order extra. We might not get another meal before we go."

"On it." She paused at the door, looking back over her shoulder to find him standing motionless and staring at her. "And, Trip?"

"Yeah?"

"No regrets." She blew him a kiss and walked

away. It wasn't an expression of undying affection, or even a promise of more to come, but it was the best she could offer... for now.

Cris watched Aria walk away, enjoying the display of bare skin and sinful curves as she departed. He almost followed her, driven by a powerful desire to wrap her in his arms and admit how deep his feelings ran. But she wasn't ready to hear that, and now was not the time for emotional confessions. She was right. They needed to stay focused on the mission.

So instead of following his heart, he retrieved his comm unit from the drawer of his bedside table and jacked in. Eric had modified the unit, turning it into a sort of digital gateway. The cheat allowed Cris more access to the cyber-sphere than his implants were supposed to have, and no one outside the team knew about it.

He took several slow breaths, centered himself, and then dove into the digital ocean that was cyberspace. Eric and the other cyber-jockeys he'd spoken to compared the experience to flying, but they were fully jacked and could experience this world in a way Cris couldn't.

For him, it was more like swimming. He had to focus on where he wanted to go and propel himself forward through what felt like a turbulent and strangely beautiful ocean. The imagery was a throwback to his youth, when one of his preferred escapes had been diving. It helped his mind cope with the strange landscape that faced him each time he went.

Data flowed like deep ocean currents, swirling around massive objects he mentally thought of as reefs and wrecks. In truth, they were governing programs, protocols, and even entire systems. He moved past them and out into the relatively quiet space beyond Babylon's network. He wouldn't be able to do this without the upgrades Eric had made to his comm unit.

It took him longer than he liked to follow the digital beacons and reach the data cache, but his frustration at his slow progress vanished when he noted the new content waiting for him. He entered more passcodes, and the cache opened. Inside was a new data packet, encrypted and tagged with Eric's personal identifiers. With any luck, the files contained the answers they needed.

He collected it, resealed the cache, and then made his way to a different nexus point. There wasn't much chance anyone was trying to track him in cyberspace, but his time in Nova Force had taught him to the value of paranoia.

As his consciousness shifted back to his body, a wave of disorientation overcame him, and he had to go through the grounding meditations Eric had taught him. It was a bit like being drunk, seasick, and experiencing sensory overload all at the same time.

Once the feeling passed, he unlocked the files and started reading.

Less than a minute later, he charged into Aria's room and interrupted her shower. She needed to see this. *Now*.

Aria turned to scowl at him, her hands raised as if to shoo him away. "Nope. Out. We do not have time for that right now."

Water coursed over her gold-tinted skin, and a fragrant steam surrounded them both. Any other day he would have abandoned good sense and joined her in the shower, kissing her until she stopped arguing with him... but not today.

They had a problem. A big one.

"You're right. We don't have time for that, but you need to make time for this." He set his comm unit down on the counter and then used both hands to activate the privacy shield he'd grabbed on his way here. Once they were contained inside the shimmering sphere, he put the generator down.

Aria eyed him curiously. They'd already scanned the place for bugs and spyware. From her perspective, there was no obvious reason why they'd need another layer of security for this conversation.

He knew differently.

"This is from Magi's newest update. Listen." He tapped his comms, and it began to read aloud the part he'd highlighted, the one summarizing Eric's findings.

Aria listened, her eyes widening and her lower lip vanishing between her teeth as she absorbed the information. Before the summary ended, she'd turned the water off and was toweling herself off with brisk efficiency.

"Absalom? That crazy voice we've been hearing belongs to Dr. Absalom?" Aria sounded equal parts disbelieving and concerned. Crispin knew exactly how she felt.

The team back on the *Malora* were almost certain that the static-filled, maniacal voice that accompanied the station's systemic failures belonged to the Gray Men's chief scientist, Dr. Jules Absalom. Since they already knew Absalom's original body was dead, that meant this had to be the doctor's digitalized consciousness. If that was the case, it was likely that what was left was deranged, fractured, and quickly unraveling.

"It would explain a few things," Crispin said. The scientist hadn't been mentally stable to begin with. He'd created VIDA and gone on to invent the technology that created the cyborgs before continuing his immoral and dangerous experiments for years, all to the benefit of the Grays.

Aria hurled her wet towel into the laundry chute with deadly accuracy and an alarming amount of force. "Why won't this bastard just die already?"

"Technically, he *did* die," Cris pointed out.

She rolled her eyes. "Exactly my point. When I said it was like the station was haunted, I didn't mean it literally, but turns out, I was right." She shooed him out of her way and then scooted past him into her bedroom.

She started dressing as he took a moment to gather up the privacy shield so they could continue the conversation. They couldn't risk Absalom's ghost overhearing anything they said.

"Maybe we can use him? He's clearly one pissed off—whatever he is," Cris said.

"Use him how? He's unstable by every definition I can think of. We don't even know for sure why he's here."

"Revenge," Cris said.

"Revenge for what? And why here? Is it VIDA?" Her skin was still damp, which made her body suit stick and catch as she tried to tug it on.

He stepped in to help. "It has to be about VIDA. I can't imagine how the *fraxx* he managed to make his way here, but if he could get this far, he could have gone anywhere. Why come to this station otherwise?"

Aria nodded sharply, her words coming out in a rush as something clicked into place for her. "That's it! That's why the AI tried to kill all Absalom's remaining clones. She was making sure he had nowhere to run."

That was so cold-bloodedly logical, Cris knew immediately that Aria had to be right. VIDA was sentient, but it was also a machine that had modeled most of its learned behavior on a dangerously unstable man and the people he worked with. "You're right. It must know there's some vestige of Absalom left and is doing all it can to kill him. He gave it too much autonomy and now it wants to be free to make its own decisions."

She turned around to face him, her expression grim. "That can't happen."

He zipped up the front of her suit and then touched her cheek. "We won't let it happen."

"Damn right we won't." She took his hand in hers and drew it away from her face, though she squeezed it once before letting him go. "Time we got to work. You said something about using the digital ghost. How?"

"By giving him a chance to get what he wants."

"You think he would work with us just to get a shot at VIDA?"

"He's been betrayed. That stings almost as much as being put in the friend zone." He'd meant it as a joke, but the moment he heard the words, he knew he'd made a mistake. It wasn't just that he'd broken one of the basic rules of investigation—the one about never letting your personal feelings affect your judgment. He'd also broken Aria's golden rule. Don't mix business with pleasure.

"Don't go there, your lordship."

Crispin raised his hands in apologetic surrender and took a deliberate step back. "I shouldn't have said that. It was a lousy joke and I am requesting a take-back. Also, you know I hate it when you call me that."

Aria's lips quirked a little at the corners. "I know. That's why I do it. And yes, you can take that back, but only if you swear to keep it professional until this is over."

He nodded and held out his hand to her. "Until exactly five minutes after the mission ends."

She was laughing as she took his hand and shook it. "You have yourself a deal."

He drew her against him and dropped his mouth to her. "Professionalism starts right after this kiss."

She didn't argue with him.

11

WHEN IT CAME to their rapidly evolving relationship, Aria didn't have all the answers, but she'd figured out one truth already. If Cris kept kissing her every time she got mad at him, she wasn't going to stay mad for long. It was an irritatingly effective method of addressing her temper.

They were both in the main lounge now, the remains of their breakfast spread out on the table. The eggs had been amazing. They were the real thing, not the protein paste version she'd always eaten, and whatever Hollandaise sauce was, she was a fan of it. The ingredients were probably worth more than her life, but surely someone had a food dispenser program that could make a decent copy. She'd look into it once they were back on the *Malora*.

If they made it that far.

Neither of them had mentioned it, but they both

knew this mission was more dangerous than anyone had expected. The appearance of Absalom's digital ghost was an unexpected variable and an unpredictable one at that.

She didn't like the idea of trying to contact Absalom, but Cris's arguments had merit. If they could enlist the ghost's help, it might increase their chances of taking VIDA down. If Eric were here, she'd have agreed it was the right call, but the ensign was a fully jacked cyber-jockey who could move through the cyber-sphere with ease. Cris's implants were more limited, and he'd only had them for a few months. A lot that could go wrong... and if it did, he would get hurt.

The problem was, she couldn't come up with a better plan.

They were working in relative silence now. Apart from the occasional comment about the food or the day's schedule, they did all their communication via their internal link while they made plans and preparations. If there was any chance that what was left of Absalom's digital consciousness was listening, they couldn't tip it off to what they were planning, and the privacy shield was a portable unit that wasn't designed to work for long periods of time.

The ghost knew too much already. Now that they knew who and what it was, the comment he'd made about "they're coming for you" made sense.

But was it warning VIDA, or threatening her? They had no way to know.

Aria was sorting and repacking what little they'd brought on board. They couldn't send everything back to the *Vixen* this early in the day. It would look odd if they transferred all their luggage back to their ship, considering they weren't scheduled to check out until after the auction. Cris had assured her that it wouldn't be noticed if they sent back one of their suitcases now. That would be the one containing everything they didn't want to leave behind. The rest could be abandoned if necessary.

She was also disassembling components of their luggage and several other items. Once she had them all, she laid them out and assembled them into something new. The grip from one of the suitcases, part of a belt buckle, several pieces that had been incorporated into the decorative collars of Crispin's vests. Separately they were benign, but once assembled correctly, they came together to form an ugly but fully functional blaster—the kind banned on Babylon Station.

Even assembled, it didn't look like a standard weapon, and the parts were made from different materials, too. It should be enough to escape notice, at least until she activated it with the extra power cell currently stashed inside Crispin's comms. The plan was for Crispin to keep the power cell with him until the last minute while Aria transported the unlikely looking firearm in a shoulder bag.

"According to your schedule, we should be on the move soon. You wanted to visit the zoo before it got too busy," she said aloud.

"Thank you, Ms. Grove. I'll be ready to leave in thirty minutes. Please arrange for housekeeping to clean up and deliver half my luggage to my ship. It will save time later."

"Of course, sir."

Over their link she sent a different message. *"Any idea how to deal with our wristbands?"*

"No. I'll check for an update before we leave in case Magi managed to figure something out, but we're almost out of time. Besides, anything he could throw together fast won't work for long. If we'd been able to get here sooner..."

That had been one of the challenges of this mission. Their window was small. Tano had sent agents to auctions here before, which meant they had to work with the arrangements he had already made. Apparently, he hadn't been interested in paying for his agent to stay any longer than was necessary. Typical of the rich... they were the cheapest beings in the galaxy when it came to spending their precious scrip.

Of course, the timing wasn't their biggest issue anymore.

"Thirty minutes doesn't leave you a lot of time to

check for an update from Magi. Not to mention you still need to see if you can track down our ghost," Aria sent through their internal link

"I'm only a mere male, but I can still multitask. I set out a lure for Absalom a while ago. It's nothing fancy, but if that thing has enough awareness left to be of any use to us, he'll want to investigate the bait I left for him. That should make finding him relatively easy."

"Finding him is one thing. Do you really think he's going to want to work with us?" She wasn't sure what she wanted his answer to be. The idea of working with the enemy, especially one that had already tried to kill several of her friends, wasn't appealing.

Crispin shrugged. "That depends on how pissed off our electronic poltergeist really is. The only way to find that out is to make contact and try to talk to it."

This was another detail Crispin hadn't been too clear on. "You really think you can do that? Talk to it? How, exactly?"

"I think I can, yeah. If it's still capable of communicating and wants to. In order to do that, I'll have to confine it so I can make a stable link between us. One that I control. That will be the tricky part," he said.

"Tricky? I'd say that's something of an understatement. Do you know how you're going to do it? Or is this more of an improv as we go situation?"

She leaned forward, fingers tangling as she clasped them in her lap. *"Were getting down to crunch time, Trip. What's our play?"*

Crispin gave her an intense look. *"It's a little logic and planning with some improv mixed in. I can only think of one way to contain that thing. I'm going to have to store it in my onboard data bank."* He tapped his temple and grimaced.

Her brain almost overloaded as a myriad of questions exploded in her head and rattled off her tongue. She started with *"Are you fraxxing kidding me?"* and ended with *"Do you have a death wish?"* She couldn't believe what she was hearing. This wasn't a half-assed plan. It was lunacy.

Chris uttered a rueful little chuckle. *"I love that you're worried about me."*

"I'm worried about the fact that you have lost your damn mind." She decided she wasn't even going to acknowledge how he'd slipped the L-word into his previous sentence. Now was not the time.

"I can do this, Ri," he told her, his voice calm and confident inside her head.

They didn't have any other choice, and she knew it. It was this insane plan or no plan at all. If this was the best they could do, then so be it. Cris knew the risks. She had to support him... even if she hated the idea. *"For the record, if you get yourself possessed by a psychotic electronic phantom, this relationship is over."*

Crispin lit up with a boyish grin that made her heart feel all quivery. *"We're in a relationship?"*

She laughed and threw up her hands in surrender. Then she leaned over and kissed him. *"Maybe. I'm not committing to anything until we both live through this. Consider it an incentive not to die."*

"I'm holding you to that."

Aria was now convinced she had the worst timing in the galaxy. But there was no point in pretending any longer. For better or for worse, there was no denying her feelings. She wasn't sure what exactly she felt for him, but it was far more than friendship or desire. She would just have to make sure they both lived long enough to find out.

Time was slipping away from them, so they tabled their conversation to focus on the mission. Cris made a few final preparations, which included moving a chair over to the room's central computer console—the one that allowed them to interact manually with the station systems if the voice recognition failed. Then they set up the privacy shield again, the shimmering walls enclosing them in a bubble that made everything feel even more intimate.

"I don't know how this is going to go. But whatever happens, try to give me as much time as you can. Even if things look like they're going wrong, unplugging me too soon will put an end to this plan," he said aloud.

"What exactly is your definition of too soon?" This plan was getting lighter on details all the time, and she wasn't happy about it.

"Honestly, I have no idea. I'm pretty sure Magi would kick my ass if he knew I was even trying this, but we don't have any other options. Give me ten minutes. If I'm not back by then, or if I appear to be in physical distress, count to five and then unplug me."

"I really, really hate this half-assed plan. Next time, I'm telling Fido to put me in charge of all planning."

He sat down on the chair, the arm with the data port lying on the armrest and his feet squarely planted on the floor. He plugged himself in and then winked at her. "I thought you liked living on the edge. See you soon." A half second later, he was gone.

It was eerie. She'd seen Eric do this more than once. His awareness entered the cyberworld, leaving his body empty and vulnerable. But that was Eric. Watching Crispin's face go slack was very different. She stood beside him, painfully aware of every second that passed and equally aware she couldn't do a damn thing to help him.

Is this what Crispin had felt when he was waiting for her to wake up from the surgery? She suspected it was. He'd done what he could to save her life, and then he'd stayed with her, without sleep or respite, until he'd been certain she was stable. Even then, it had taken an order from their commander to send him away, but the fact he hadn't come back to be there when she'd woken up had stung. But now she understood why. Guilt. Of all the emotions she'd expected him to feel, that hadn't even been on the list.

More time passed. He'd been gone seven minutes now, and every second had dragged on for an eternity. She couldn't do anything but stay at his side and wait. It was torturous. She didn't like being helpless.

Another thirty seconds passed, and she caught herself grinding her teeth. "Calm down. He's fine," she murmured to herself.

Then his chest heaved, and he sucked in a deep breath. At first, she thought he was coming back to reality, but then everything went wrong. Instead of waking up, Cris thrashed in the chair, his head snapping back and forth while his hands gripped the armrests so tightly the fabric tore.

Aria managed to count to three before she gave in and tugged the jack out of his port. Screw counting to five. Something was wrong!

She expected him to relax now that he was unplugged, but he didn't. The sharp head movements continued and his mouth was twisted into a grimace that might have been pain. She couldn't tell for certain.

She stepped in front of him, straddling his thighs and catching hold of his wrists with her hands. "Trip! You need to come back now. Right now!" She squeezed his arms tightly and hoped her words got through. Eric had warned the team not to touch him while he was jacked in. The unexpected contact could disrupt his focus or startle him into a defensive response. She had to risk it, though. It was the only thing she could think to do.

To her relief, it seemed to work. Cris slowly relaxed and his head stopped whipping from side to side. He uttered a low groan, so at least he was breathing. That was something.

"Cris?" she verbally nudged him.

His eyes fluttered open, and he gave her a groggy half-smile. "Hey there. Miss me?"

She growled and let go of his arms. "I'm not answering that question until you answer mine. What the hell happened? Are you okay? Did you get the ghost?" She frowned at that last query. It sounded so wrong to be talking about ghosts on a serious mission.

"The plan worked... mostly. What's left of the crazy doctor went for my bait but tried to bolt once I showed up. Led me on a merry chase through the system, but eventually I caught him. He wasn't thrilled about that part."

"I could tell. Your neck is going to hurt for a bit the way you were whipping it around, and we are definitely going to get a bill for the furniture you trashed."

"Trashed?" He looked around in confusion.

"You survived trapping Absalom. The chair didn't."

He eyed the gouges in the armrests with surprise. "Huh. I thought the fight was all in the digital realm. Good thing we're not paying for this room. Huh?"

"I can't imagine our employers agreeing to expense this level of luxury." She stepped back and offered him her hand. "Up you get. We've got more to do." She paused and then added, "Unless you're not okay? Do you need a minute?"

He took her hand but rose without her help, his eyes dancing with amusement. "I'm fine. Allow me to prove it to you." He tugged her into his arms and kissed her, branding her mouth with his lips. All hunger and heat. She should be resisting, reminding him they had work to do, but she couldn't do it. Not when she needed this so much. Needed to know he was really okay. Losing him as a friend would have hurt her deeply. Losing him completely would destroy her.

That knowledge flared as brightly as a star, searing away the last of her doubts and excuses. She loved him. Stars help her. She'd been in love with him for years. Somewhere in the back of her mind, she heard her mother laugh. "...knew you'd figure it out eventually, starshine." Her mother had always left her to figure things out on her own instead of helping her right away. She'd heard those words so many times growing up. She had to blink away the tears that stung her eyes before Cris saw them and misunderstood.

They'd had too many misunderstandings already. It was time to do things differently... if they survived the next few hours.

Ending their kiss wasn't easy, but Cris managed it eventually. After years of imagining what it would be like to have her in his arms any time he wanted, the reality had turned out to be even better... and far more addictive.

He took a moment to refresh himself, restyling his hair and changing his shirt when he noticed the one he had on was rumpled.

All the while, he could feel the captured presence inside him. It was infuriated at being caught, but it wasn't actively fighting him anymore. He'd left the data he'd used to lure

Absalom accessible so he could read and absorb it. It contained everything they knew about VIDA's vault and what she'd been up to since his physical death. Now, he unlocked another part of the data, the one that revealed their plan to take down the rogue AI. Along with it was an offer. They'd get Absalom access to the vault in exchange for the destruction of VIDA.

It took his temporary hitchhiker almost a minute to reply. What was left of what had once been one of the most brilliant minds in the galaxy was now little more than a collection of scattered memories, cunning, and instinct held together purely by his hatred-fueled fixation on VIDA.

When the answer came back, it was a single word. "Yes."

"Absalom has agreed to our plan," Cris announced over their link. Trusting the doctor's electronic echo was risky, but it was the best chance they had of success. Attacking the AI by themselves would take too long, especially since they hadn't found a way around the wristbands.

Damn it. He'd forgotten he still needed to check one last time for an update from Eric. He'd have to do it quickly... He stopped mid-thought as reality raised a red flag. He couldn't do that now. Not when he had Absalom stored inside his head. He couldn't take the chance that he might renege and escape. It wasn't likely, but he couldn't risk it. If the ghost managed to find his way to the *Malora*... He didn't want to even think about it.

He re-entered the main room and reactivated the

privacy shield before speaking aloud. "I had to make a slight change to the plan."

Her lips thinned, and she watched him with calm concern. "Why?"

"I failed to consider what could happen if I gave Absalom the opportunity to track down the *Malora* via cyberspace. If I open that data cache..."

She winced. "Right. That didn't occur to me, either. Good thing we know how to improvise."

"We'll make this work. Step one is to get through the door. Step two is to reunite Absalom and his errant creation."

She chimed in before he could finish. "And step three is to run like hell."

He clapped his hands once and nodded. "Exactly. Ready to go?"

"As I'll ever be." She caught his hand and squeezed it quickly. "Don't get dead. Okay?"

"I won't if you won't." He raised their hands and pressed a kiss to her knuckles, his gaze never leaving hers. "I'm not going anywhere, Ri."

Her reply warmed his soul like sunlight pouring into a dimly lit room. "Neither am I. So let's get this done so we can talk about what happens next."

12

THE ZOO WASN'T AS busy as it had been the day before. In fact, the entire station seemed quieter this morning. It was probably because everyone was still sleeping or enjoying their breakfast in a civilized fashion after a night of exhaustive social posturing and watching each other for any signs of weakness.

He really didn't miss that life. The first night he'd been free of it he'd had the best sleep he'd had since his father had decided he was old enough to be indoctrinated into the family business... politics and power.

The lack of visitors was a two-edged blade. On the one hand, fewer eyes were around to notice what he and Aria were up to. On the other hand, it meant they were conspicuous simply by being there. That awareness left him feeling exposed.

Despite the tension of the moment, or maybe

because of it, he was more aware of Aria. She was a steady presence, alert and ready to take on anything and anyone. She was as much a predator as any animal in this zoo—lithe, graceful, and dangerously beautiful.

They worked together like a well-oiled machine despite the fact that there was almost no communication between them. They didn't need to check in with each other. They each knew what the other was thinking and how they'd react to any situation. They made their way toward the entrance to the vaults, adrenaline and desire heightening his senses. He could smell the soap she'd used in the shower and the whisper of her clothes as she moved.

Was this the way they could have been all this time? Had they been missing out on something so special because they'd been afraid to try? And it had been their choice. Aria might have made the call, but he'd never challenged her decisions, and maybe he should have.

Or maybe not. His regret slowly gave way to the realization that this wasn't something that could be rushed. He knew her so well not because of their chemistry but because he'd been with her through tests and trials over the last three years. This was something that had grown slowly and if he'd pushed too hard then, it wouldn't be the same now. Their friendship had deepened and evolved over time.

She'd been right not to rush, though her reasons

had been all wrong. Not that he was going to mention that to her right now... or any time soon. He'd have to make sure they were alone in a room with no sharp objects. Maybe in a few years. He had no doubts they'd still be together. He was going to spend the rest of his life with her. Aria Jessop. The woman he loved.

They passed the Nantari rhino exhibit and he took a moment to glance through one of the small viewing windows set into this part of the wall.

Aria stopped and took up a guard position at his back.

"Only the holographic rhinos are out today," he said. "It seems they have learned from yesterday's mistakes."

"Yes, sir," Aria said. Through their link she added *"I wonder where they put the two real ones. One of the shuttle bays, maybe?"*

Cris allowed himself a small smile before turning away. *"Can you imagine the face of some hapless pilot who entered the wrong bay and found themselves facing two beasts almost the size of their shuttle?"*

Although the carnivorous fish display was their primary goal, he had to make it look like he was interested in finishing the entire zoo experience. So, as much as it chafed him, they had to waste time working their way through the part of the zoo he hadn't seen yesterday on their way to the massive tank.

They reached that part of the zoo eventually, and his pulse ticked up a notch as they drew ever closer to their goal.

Something was ominous about the aquatic area. It might have been simply that the light here flickered and wavered constantly, creating shadows and the illusion of movement all around them. The air was different here. Despite all the filtration systems it had a feeling of dampness to it accompanied by the subtle scents of distant oceans and marshlands.

The contents of the tanks were fascinating, and any other day he'd have spent hours observing the creatures inside. Today, though, it was all he could do to pause long enough to make it look like he was interested.

The glass on the tanks was interactive, allowing the visitors to touch it and call up descriptions and images of the various animals inside. Schools of brightly colored fish swarmed and darted in schools. More fish lurked on the sandy bottom or hid inside the artificial reefs. He didn't recognize them all, which wasn't a surprise given the tanks were partitioned off so all creatures from different planets could co-exist side by side.

As he watched, a tiny octopus shot past him, its brilliant blue rings pulsing in time to its movements. He stared at it in shock. "Aren't those supposed to be extinct? Earth's oceans are nothing but toxic sludge."

Aria turned to look as he activated the tank's

display. He'd been right. It was a blue-ringed octopus, but it was only a hologram. He'd only known about it from the stories one of his tutors had told him about all the dangerous animals that had once roamed the Earth.

The path they were on curved just ahead, leading them into a new part of the exhibit. Here the light was darker and the shadows cast by the fish far, far larger. An animal more than three meters long swam by them, its long tail lashing slowly from side to side.

A short time later, the same fish appeared again, and this time it matched their pace, its pure black eyes watching intently.

He stopped to look at it more closely, noting the streamlined shape and the scars that marked its mottled gray skin.

"Remind you of anyone?" Aria asked via their link.

"Trin before she's had her ja'kreesh in the morning?"

"Well, now that you mention it, yes, but I meant someone else. Visualize it in bright caftan," she replied.

Now he saw it. The dark predator eyes and effortless grace. *"Ketris. I wonder if she knows she's got kin on the station."*

Aria made a soft sound of amusement and shot him a sidelong look. *"I dare you to tell her that."*

"Not a chance. We're taking enough risks already. We'll have to warn her before we breach VIDA's vault. That's more than enough contact for me." Ketris was an apex predator, and at the moment they were swimming in her waters.

He looked at the shark again. It was a living fossil, a remnant from another age of history. He'd never expected to see one in the flesh, and despite their current situation, he'd never forget this moment.

Aria tapped the tank and information on the creature appeared. It was a female tiger shark, cloned from one of the last animals held in captivity after Earth's entire ecosystem was already sliding into total collapse.

The fish swam in slow circles, never letting him out of its sight. Logically he knew it was no threat to him, but the part of him that still ran on instinct was insisting it was time he moved on, far away from the predator taking an uncomfortable interest in him.

Aria must have noticed it too because she sent another message through their link. *"I think she likes you, Trip. Must have heard what you said about being a fellow predator yesterday."*

"Ha-ha. Very funny. She's just bored."

He moved on and the shark followed him. He lengthened his stride and the *fraxxing* thing sped up, too.

"Oh yeah, she likes you. Should I be jealous?"

He should have kept up the easy banter they had going, but his mouth got ahead of his common sense. *"No female in the universe compares to you. Never has. Never will."*

Their link went silent. For the next thirty seconds there was no sound but the ambient gurgle of the tanks' pumps and the steady beat of their footsteps.

When she finally answered him, he had to fight to keep from grinning.

"It's hard to do my job when you keep distracting me with compliments."

"Are you telling me to stop?"

Another pause, only a few seconds this time. *"No."*

Aria caught up to him and pointed up to the bridge they needed to reach. "I believe you can get the best view from up there, sir."

"I believe you are correct, Ms. Grove." He moved toward the stairs leading up to the viewing area. This was where things got complicated.

Aria followed Cris up the narrow staircase that led to the observation area overlooking the aquatic exhibits. Up here, the air was warm and humid, creating an odd little microclimate and making the atmosphere feel thick and close.

Most of the tanks were left open on top. It probably made maintenance easier, but it meant they were now standing above a large tank of warm, salty water full of creatures with big teeth and an appetite for fresh meat. Not ideal.

Worse, the floor was transparent. Her toes curled inside her boots as she looked down into the depths of the water below. Despite all her training in zero-G the view was unsettling. This wasn't space. Gravity still pulled her downward, but her brain didn't trust the transparent floor to support her. She suspected the choice of materials had been intentional, not only to enhance the experience for visitors but to make sure no one lingered too long near the hidden door to the vault.

The access door had been made to look like just another wall panel, decorated in the same pale blue and green tiles that were everywhere in this part of the zoo. It was easy to see with her optical implant, but it was unlikely anyone else would notice it.

She followed Cris onto the bridge, doing her best to ignore the way the hairs on the back of her neck rose as they traversed the clear floor. It didn't help that they were both aware that this system was designed to retract. The last thing they needed was to be trapped on this side of the tank.

The walls were the same transparent material as the floor. They rose high enough to ensure no one went over the side of the viewing area and into the tank below—either accidentally or on purpose. Given the kind of clientele that visited the station, she wondered how many attempted murders had happened here before they'd added the sides. It also turned the bridge into a killing field.

She resisted the urge to toy with her wristband. Was someone watching them right now? Making sure they didn't do anything unexpected? Would an alarm trip when they passed through a door they shouldn't have access to? She had no way to know, but they were assuming that was a likely scenario. That's why she was armed. Or would be, once Cris handed her the power supply he carried.

Hopefully Crispin would be able to hack the door quickly enough they'd avoid notice. Every second they went undetected increased their chances of completing their mission.

None of the pressure or concern they both had to be feeling showed in Cris's expression. He strolled along the bridge with calm self-assurance, though she noticed he glanced down more than once. The reason was obvious. The shark was still following him. Now it was below them, circling just below the surface, her dorsal fin slicing through the water as she moved.

When they got back to the rest of the team, she was going to have fun telling the story of the shark with a crush on Cris. It would be worth at least a few drinks and possibly a new nickname for him. Shark bait maybe? She'd have to enlist Eric's help with that. Nicknames were one of his specialties.

Once they reached the far side of the bridge, she did a quick pass around the smaller platform as if she were checking for threats to her employer. It gave her a chance to do an up-close scan of the door. The access panel was hidden, too, but from what she could see the cover was very basic. It wasn't locked. You simply had to know where it was so you could slide it aside. It was too bad Tano Farr had been too paranoid to trust even Babylon's vaunted security. If he had a vault here, they would already have the code to get in.

Cris moved around, watching the fish while she did her sweep, and then the two of them wandered over to a good vantage point. He took a seat and she took up position to his left, standing so she had a good view of the bridge and anyone who might approach. It also meant the cameras she'd been able to identify would all be blocked by either her body or his, which gave Crispin the opportunity to slip her the power supply he'd been carrying.

She placed it in her bag without being seen. She'd power up her weapon at the last possible moment. The longer the gun was active, the higher the chance that it would be detected and trigger an alert.

Cris stretched out his legs in front of him with one booted foot crossed over the other. "This feels a bit like last night's party," he said aloud. Through their link he said something quite different. *"I'm going to get in contact with our ghost again."*

"At least these predators are quieter." She wanted to turn toward him and glare to demand what the hell he was thinking. She managed to stay where she was, though her hands tightened into fists at her sides. Why would he want to connect with that *thing* again? The more he interacted with that thing inside his head, the greater the chance something went wrong. *"Why?"* she sent to him.

He shifted his weight and looked down at the dark shape of the shark swimming beneath them. *"Because this is Absalom. He knew the access code to this door when he was alive. Maybe he still remembers it. Even if he doesn't, he's been lurking in this station's systems and rattling various electronic cages for at least a week. If he has the code, it would save us a great deal of time."*

He was right, but she still didn't like the idea. *"If you have another seizure out here it won't save time. It will draw all sorts of attention."*

"That won't happen again. Absalom knows this is his last chance for revenge. He's not so far gone he'll forget that."

"You'd better be right about this. If you get zapped again, I am totally tossing your unconscious ass to your new girlfriend below."

"Noted. Don't worry, Ri. I plan to be around to

annoy you for years to come."

Before today, she would have denied being worried at all, but that ship had left orbit already, and it wasn't coming back. *"Do it. I'll watch your back."*

"You always do." Crisp went eerily still. It was almost the way the cyborgs did it, like the body went into standby mode, waiting. This time his face didn't go completely slack, though. Instead, he looked distracted and distant, like he was thinking hard about something that had taken up all his awareness.

A fish breeched the surface of the water in one of the tanks, the flicker of silver catching her attention. When it dove back under the waves, the water erupted into a froth of foam and splashing that only lasted a few seconds. A large shadow darted away, and the tank went quiet again.

"I hate it when the universe decides to get dramatic," she muttered to herself.

"Hmm?" Cris's query wasn't more than a soft hum, but some of the knots in her belly loosened when she heard him.

"You with me again?" she asked over their channel.

"I am, and I have the code."

She brushed her hand over the pocket with the power supply and then touched the bag that held the blaster. It was time. *"Then let's do this."*

Cris stood, stretched, and then did what looked like an aimless ramble around the circumference of the platform before stopping by the door they needed to open. The plan was for him to lean up against the wall as he appeared to adjust the fit of one shoe while she stood guard, using her body to shield him from view as he punched in the code.

At least, that *had* been the plan.

Instead, he turned to her with a wicked smile on his lips. "Come here, Ms. Grove."

"Sir?"

"Here. Now." He pointed to the floor in front of him, his tone one of pure dominance and command.

"Yes, sir." She walked over to him, adding an extra bit of sway to her hips with each step.

"Do you know what I want to do now, Ms. Grove?" he asked in a low, husky voice.

An unexpected thrill of desire went through her, making her clit throb and her bodysuit suddenly seem a size too small.

"No sir." She dropped her voice to a seductive purr. "Maybe you should tell me exactly what you want from me, sir."

The ploy might have been fake, but the heat in Cris's eyes was very real. "Find somewhere private and do very bad things to you." He raised his hand, letting his fingers trail down her cheek, to her jaw, and then her throat. His hand closed slightly, and the next thing she knew they had traded places so that her back was to the wall.

If anyone else had tried this, she'd have resisted.

But this was Cris, and though she still wasn't sure what the hell he was doing, she trusted him. More than that... she was enjoying this display of dominance.

Not that she was going to tell him that.

He kept one hand on her throat as his lips crashed down on hers. His touch was possessive, his mouth demanding. She gave herself over to the moment, surrendering to him, and the groan that rose from his chest told her that he was as affected as she was... and just as insane.

Maybe that was why she'd resisted all this time. Not because it might mess up her career, but because she knew that if she let him into her heart, she'd never let him go.

Her hands glided over his shoulders to lock behind his head, pulling him in for a deeper kiss. She nipped his lower lip, and she felt his cock swell in response. Somehow he managed to kiss her senseless and still hold on to enough focus to open the panel and punch in the code Absalom's echo had given him.

The door slid open with a barely audible hiss and they tumbled through it, still wrapped around each other.

They stayed that way until the door closed and the panel glowed red, indicating it was sealed and locked. She let go of him and grabbed for the bag still slung over her shoulder, her free hand already pulling the power supply out of her pocket. She had the blaster out in a matter of seconds and slapped the power source into place.

"Give me your wrist. We need to get these wrist bands off," Cris said.

She was already turning toward him when another voice spoke, this one low and dangerous. "We warned you not to do that. If you cut those off, you're both dead."

Well, *fraxx*.

13

Cris's hand moved to his hip on reflex, his fingers closing over empty air. No blaster.

Aria drew her weapon and aimed down the corridor as they both moved to the first place that offered some cover, a small junction box that jutted out from the wall. His first instinct was to push Aria into the more protected position, but he knew better. She'd resent it. Not to mention she was the one with the gun.

Someone tall stepped out of the shadows and Cris had a moment of recognition. It was Ramon, the man assigned as Aria's liaison on the station. What the hell was he doing here?

"Ramon? What are you doing here?" Aria asked, her tone crisp and cool as an autumn wind.

The big man scowled at them. "I work here. What's your excuse for being in an unauthorized part of the station? How did you get the access code? Your employer doesn't use Babylon's storage facilities."

Ramon wasn't armed. While his face was still partially in shadow and hard to read, Cris was sure the other man looked more nervous than angry. Something odd was going on. He just wasn't sure what it was.

"I'm working more than one contract right now. I got the code from my second client," Cris said. It was more or less the truth, so long as you looked at the situation sideways and squinted a little.

"Who?" Ramon demanded as he folded his arms across his chest.

"Does that matter?" Aria stood up and lowered the blaster, though she didn't put it away. "We're here. You're here. The only question that matters is—what happens now?"

Ramon's jaw tightened, his shoulders stiffening. Before he could answer, though, another figure stepped out of the shadows.

Synda.

She touched Ramon's arm lightly and his head snapped around to stare at her. "I told you to stay out of sight."

"And I told you we could trust them. We don't have time for this. We have to move or we're all going to get caught."

"Caught?" Aria asked.

"Caught how?" Cris added.

Synda gestured vaguely around them. "The cameras in this area are rebooting. They'll be active again soon, though." She tipped her head to one side, silver eyes gleaming. "I know you're not who you claim to be. I also know you're not like the other guests. Whatever you're planning to do, we can help you. But there's a price."

Aria nodded, her eyes never leaving Synda's. "What's the price?"

The little Pheran female raised her chin, and in a voice stronger and clearer than anything he'd heard from her before said, "When you leave, you have to take us with you."

Ramon's arm caught her around the waist, and he pulled her into his side. "That wasn't the plan, little one."

Synda smiled up at the human male, and for a moment she let the mask of a demure and willing servant fall away, revealing a determined female very much in love. "Sending me away while you stayed here was *your* plan. My plan always included you. This child will need their father."

Aria turned to look at him, a warm light in her silver eyes. "Haven?" she asked.

He wanted to say no. This mission was dangerous enough already. Having a couple of civilians with them—and a pregnant one at that—was not even in the same solar system as anything resembling a good idea. But they couldn't leave them here, either.

"*Do you trust them?*" he sent over their link. He knew she'd understand he wanted to know if she'd seen anything in their body language or wording that would indicate they were lying.

"*They're not hiding anything except their fear.*"

That was all he needed to know. "Haven," he agreed, naming the colony of Vardarians and cyborgs where Aria had recovered. The place was full of good beings who'd be happy to take on two more refugees of a cruel and uncaring galaxy. Hell, the two liaisons probably had a good bit of valuable intelligence they could share with Nova Force.

"Is that a yes?" Synda asked, her voice soft again.

Aria's smile was kind but knowing. "It is. But I think you already sensed that. You're one of the *m'bara*. Aren't you? A Pheran empath."

Ramon snarled and stepped in front of his female protectively. Cris did the same, instinct demanding he match the other man move for move.

Synda and Aria both muttered something unintelligible and pushed past the two men. "We don't have time for this, Ramon," Synda scolded her male.

"And I don't have the patience," Aria added, shooting Cris an irritated look. "Nor do I need rescuing."

"You are hell on my ego, woman." He'd meant to

send that via their link, but it came out of his mouth instead.

Ramon's brows quirked up and Synda laughed softly as she looked between them. "I'm glad you two got that sorted out."

"It's a work in progress." Aria made a show of putting away the blaster before moving closer to the other pair.

"You get us to our objective, and we'll get you out of here. You have my word," Aria said and then held out her hand to Synda.

The Pheran took Aria's hand and then froze, her silver eyes wide with shock. Aria must have dropped her mental walls and allowed the female to sense her real self. The *m'bara* weren't telepathic, but those born with the ability could learn a great deal about them even without being able to read their thoughts directly.

Cris knew what was in Aria's heart. She was strong, focused, determined and kind.

That's why he loved her.

In a matter of seconds their new allies had whipped out two sets of electronic keys and removed the bands from his and Aria's wrists. They traded them for another pair, these the same dull grey and red as the ones Ramon and Synda wore.

"Staff passes?" Aria asked.

"These are temporary ones, usually given to the staff of our most important guests," Ramon's voice hardened. "Can't have the lowly servants wandering the halls where just anyone might run across them. They use the same back passages we do."

"Invisible," Aria said.

"Out of sight and out of mind until needed," Cris added.

Synda straightened and smiled. "Soon, we'll be out of their sight forever."

"It won't take us long to do what we need to do. But if we can use these passages to stay out of sight, it would increase our chances of getting out of here in one piece." Cris glanced at Synda and then at her male. "If things go to hell, can you run fast enough to get yourself out of here?"

"I will make sure she does," Ramon said.

"Then let's get this over with. The sooner we're done here, the faster we can leave this overly opulent corner of hell." Aria fixed Ramon with a steady stare. "Which way to the vaults?"

"Whose?" he asked without hesitation.

"Dr. Jules Absalom."

Synda and Ramon froze, mouths open, eyes suddenly wary. "Why?" Ramon demanded.

"Because we need to deal with something in that vault," Cris said.

"Before it deals with us," Aria said.

"This way." Ramon caught Synda by the hand and then led them into the dimly lit corridor. The lights activated as they approached each section and dimmed again behind them, leaving them surrounded by perpetual shadow.

The four of them made very little noise as they hurried along, but every scuff of a foot or hiss of breath seemed overly loud in this place. They all felt a sense of danger here, a lingering threat Cris knew wasn't directed at them. He'd been in enough prisons to recognize what this was, an opulent palace maintained by an army of staff that scurried through these corridors like rats in an inescapable maze.

They had to stop at each junction as Ramon used his higher-level access to clear the way forward. Given who they were, many of the station's clients insisted that all security features, including the cameras, be deactivated before they'd move on. It meant that every trip to the vaults was a longer process and required a liaison to accompany them, but they were assured of total privacy.

Absalom's vault was at the end of the corridor. "This is it," Ramon said. "The cameras in this area will be deactivated for three minutes. If you need more time than that, I'll have to reset them again. More than two resets will trigger alerts."

"We'll be as fast as we can," Aria said.

"We shouldn't need more than two minutes. Then we get the hell out of here as fast as possible."

"How long until the explosion goes off?" Synda asked. It took Cris a moment to realize she thought that was what they were here to do.

"No explosions. I just need to deliver a package." He couldn't tell them more than that.

Synda's stance relaxed. "Oh good. I was afraid helping you might put the others at risk. This was..." she swallowed hard before continuing. "This wasn't an easy decision."

"I can't promise no risk, but it was never our intention to destroy the station or anyone on it."

Aria picked up where he'd left off. "We'll explain once we're away from this place." Ramon and Synda nodded in understanding. Some things were better left unsaid, like the name of the organization he and Aria answered to.

He tapped the part of his implant where the echo of Absalom lurked and let him know they were close. Absalom went into a frenzy, filling Cris's head with static and electrical discharges that made it hard to think.

"Stop." He told his hitchhiker. "If you kill me, you'll never get to her."

Absalom quieted, but he could still sense its agitation.

He walked past the others to the keypad. Once there, he tapped in the long code that their source had provided, checking in with Absalom before hitting the final character.

The pad turned green and the door slid open. They were in.

Aria peeked past him. "That's it?" she asked.

There wasn't much to see. The vault was barely the size of his quarters back on the *Malora*. The walls were the same nondescript beige as the halls they'd traversed on their way here with no decorations or amenities. Just a single chair sat in front of a large console and an armored shell he assumed contained VIDA.

"Not much to look at," Cris agreed.

Ramon shrugged. "Every vault is decorated as per the client's specifications. Most clients prefer more luxury than this, but Absalom was always different."

"You've met him?" Aria asked.

"We've met *them*," Synda said, her voice barely a whisper. "The same but different."

Of course. Synda's abilities would allow her to sense the truth about Absalom and his clones. Once they were away from here, he'd ask how one of her kind had been allowed to leave their home planet. Most never did. At least, not without their owners.

Cris's mind was already on the task ahead. His role was simple enough. What he hadn't told Aria was how risky it would be. Trying to trap Absalom's ghost would have earned him a reprimand from Dax and an ass-kicking from Kurt. If they knew the risk he was taking this time, they'd likely throw him out an airlock and claim it was to save him the trouble of killing himself.

The thing was, there was a good chance he was

going to beat them to it. The only way to transfer Absalom into VIDA was to create a link and let the ghost use him as a conduit. The problem was that was a two-way connection. While Absalom was leaving, there was a good chance VIDA would try to kill Cris. She'd nearly managed it with Eric already, and he was far better at protecting himself than Cris was.

If he did this, there was a chance he wasn't coming home from this mission. Too bad it was the only plan he had. Nothing else they had would make a dent in the armor protecting their target, and Absalom had a far better chance of taking down his creation from the inside than Cris would.

"Where do you want us?" Ramon asked.

"You two stay out here. We'll leave the door open, but if anyone comes, duck inside, out of sight. It might get messy in here, though. So only as a last resort," Aria said.

Two pairs of brows rose in question, but Aria didn't elaborate.

Cris stepped inside and sat down in the single chair even before he had the data-jack out of his pocket. "Speaking of messy, I think it's time to give our ally of the dubious morals a heads up. She won't appreciate it if all hell breaks loose and we didn't warn her first."

Aria nodded crisply. "I'll do that now. I wouldn't like to be on Ketris's bad side. I like my career."

"And I like breathing," Cris said.

By the time she'd sent the message, he was already plugged in and ready to go. Absalom was tearing around his head like a whirlwind, aware his moment of revenge was at hand.

Cris had one thing to do first. He turned to look at Aria. Her jaw was tight and her expression stony. It was the mask of a professional soldier, the one that showed no hint of her feelings and let her keep her distance from anything that could distract her from the mission at hand.

It wasn't the way he wanted to see her. Not if this was the last time. "Ri," he spoke her name softly.

"Don't."

He caught her hand and tugged her closer. "Whatever happens next, get clear. Get home, and make sure they name the baby after me. You got it?"

"Do it yourself." She bit off each word, her eyes not meeting his.

"That's the plan."

She relaxed the slightest bit. "Then we don't need to continue this conversation. Get this over with so we can get the *fraxx* out of here."

"Is that an order?" he asked.

"Damn right it is. We might be the same rank, but I've got seniority." She shot him a dark look. "And if this is as dangerous as I'm starting to suspect it is, I've got another one for you. Come back alive or I will kill you myself."

He raised her hand to his lips and kissed it. "I love you, too."

Then he opened the link between him and VIDA and was flung into the middle of a battle his mind could barely comprehend. It was like opening the cage of a dangerous predator, throwing another feral beast inside, and then trying to slam the gate shut before either of them escaped. Something huge, dark, and powerful flowed toward him, a seething ball of hatred and fury.

Absalom flung himself at her with a shriek that shouldn't have been possible, but it tore through Cris's mind, shattering his senses and leaving him stunned and vulnerable. VIDA and Absalom tore at each other, but the AI was massive in comparison to its creator, and part of it reached Cris. Pain flowed through him, electricity making his muscles flex and tear as neurons misfired and cells were destroyed in the onslaught.

With the last of his strength, he cut off the connection, leaving the madman and his demented creation to destroy each other.

Then a different kind of darkness rose around him, and everything went quiet. His last thoughts were of Aria. His beautiful goddess of war.

They should have had more time.

~

She was going to kill him.

The *fraxxing* fool had known how risky this was and hadn't told her. Now he was unconscious, the skin around his data port red and swollen from burns. A quick scan with her cybernetic eye told her that he had first and second degree burns on his arm, some of them internal. The attack had incapacitated him, but he wasn't dead… not yet, anyway. Once they were away from here, she was going to kill him slowly for telling her he loved her and then vanishing before she had time to respond.

"You asshole!" she hissed at him as she tried to shake him awake. "Open your eyes and move your ass, your lordship. We have places to be!"

Cris groaned, one eye flickering open. "I thought we agreed you weren't going to call me that anymore. Also, ow."

"I never agreed to any such thing, and after that stunt, I might come up with a whole new list of annoying things to call you. Idiot. Fool. Son of a poxy stardragon."

Both of his eyes were open now. "Is this your way of saying you were worried?"

"No. Yes. Maybe. I'm too mad to be certain right now. So get your ass out of that chair and move. If you die before we get to the *Vixen*, I won't have to tell you I love you."

He grinned and pushed himself out of the chair

with a low groan that told her he was in pain. "As motivations go, that's the best I've ever heard."

He caught her hand and pulled her in for a brief, hot kiss that was little more than a crash of lips and a sear of blistering heat. "Just remember who said it first."

"Yeah, while you were proving yet again that you need a permanent bodyguard to keep you from doing stupid things."

"You volunteering?" he asked.

"Not until I hear the details. I expect danger pay and a benefits package. You're going to be a lot of work."

He laughed and headed for the door. "If you do agree to all negotiations while naked, I think you'll find I can be a very generous man."

Her retort was drowned out by a screech of electronic feedback closely followed by a power surge that made the lights flicker and the gravity destabilize for a few disorienting seconds.

"What the *fraxx* is happening now?" Aria demanded.

Cris's expression went distant for several long seconds. When he came back, his face folded into lines of concern and determination. "I *fraxxed* up. We need to go. Now!"

She didn't bother asking what had gone wrong. They'd have time for that later. She caught hold of his wrist in one hand and ran for the door.

Synda and Ramon waited outside, both of them tense and pacing as the emergency lights flashed and a calm, automated voice advised all beings in the area to return to their rooms or the nearest designated sanctuary locations.

"What do we do now?" Ramon demanded.

"This is the part where we run like hell," Aria replied. "Which way?"

Synda didn't bother to point. She just turned and ran. They all followed her. Aria kept a grip on Cris, pulling him along with her at speeds he couldn't have managed on his own.

When Synda slowed down, Ramon scooped her into his arms and kept running. When he started to falter, Aria grabbed his hand, too. The power fluctuations were disorienting, as were the random shifts in gravity. Showers of sparks rained down on them from blown transformers and power couplings.

It didn't take her long to realize that while the entire station was being affected, the worst of it seemed to be focused on them.

Fraxx. Fraxx. Fraxx. What was after them? Absalom, VIDA, or both? Not that it mattered much. One was just as dangerous as the other.

They dashed down identical corridors, guided by Ramon's breathless directions. The two liaisons were trim and lithe, but they clearly didn't do much cardio. Their lack of endurance told her they weren't well-fed, either. They'd probably enjoy decimating the *Vixen's* amply stocked galley once they got aboard and away from the station.

A scream of female fury exploded from the speakers. The wordless shriek made the hair on the back of Aria's neck rise.

"Bitch!" another voice cried, this one crackling with static and madness. "You did this to me."

"What is that?" Synda asked, her voice high and sharp with fear.

"Two very good reasons to get the *fraxx* out of here," Cris said.

Aria risked a quick glance at him and noted that his burned arm was curled against his side. It had to be agonizing, but the only sign of it on his face was a tightness around his mouth and a few deepened lines under his eyes.

"There!" Ramon rasped between panting breaths. "Second door on the left will take us into the lobby. That's as far as these back corridors go."

Damn. She'd hoped they'd have a back way to access the docking area itself. So far they hadn't seen another soul, and she'd wanted to keep it that way. They slowed just a few steps before they reached the door. The last thing they needed was to draw attention by exploding into the lobby like they were being chased by a herd of crazed Nantari rhinos.

All of them paused just long enough to smooth out their hair and clothes and then fell into a single line formation with Cris leading. She followed a few paces behind with their liaisons following up the rear. They kept their breathing steady, their pace unhurried, and stepped into the lobby as if they had every right to be there.

They shouldn't have bothered.

The entire lobby was in chaos. The grav-plates controlling the waterfall were malfunctioning, allowing the water to crash down one minute and fly back into the air the next. Beings fled in panic as the grav-plates in other areas fluctuated, sending people soaring high into the air while others were pinned to the deck, trying to crawl to safety.

Cris spun around to meet Ramon's eyes. "Get to the *Twisted Vixen*. Docking bay eight. Passcode to enter is 996999. Find a chair and strap yourselves in. Do not stop for anything, not even us."

Ramon nodded, but Synda didn't look convinced. "Without you, the ship won't leave, though."

"It will. I'll make sure of it. The two of you are getting off this station no matter what."

Aria heard the truth in his words and felt a rush of love and deep admiration for him. This was the man she'd fallen in love with. The one who had walked away from a life of unimaginable luxury to take care of those who needed his help.

"Go. If anyone asks where you're going, tell them we've requested an escort back to our ship due to the current situation." The order rolled off Cris's lips like he'd been born to command. The two civilians reacted instantly and made straight for the air barriers that separated the lobby from the docks.

She made sure her blaster was concealed in her bag and fell in behind Crispin as they hurried through the panicked crowd, making sure to avoid the areas in gravitational flux. Once they stumbled into a high-gravity area. She managed to haul them back out again, though it taxed her cybernetics and added new damage to her already aching arms.

VIDA shrieked again, this time with more pain than fury in the tones, along with an undernote of fear. The AI was afraid.

Good.

That meant the demented echo of the doctor was a match for it. It meant they had a chance to get away.

Synda reached the air barriers first with Ramon right behind her. They were going to make it!

Then, the lights went out and all she could hear were panicked cries and the ear-shattering roar of several tons of water crashing down on the deck.

A handful of emergency lights illuminated the area just enough for her ocular implant to work. She spotted the air barrier, caught hold of Cris, planted her feet and flung him toward the one thing that could stop the wall of water rushing toward them.

In the faint light she saw his face, his mouth open

and eyes wild, but there was too much noise for her to make out what he said.

She wanted to believe it was her name.

As the wave smashed into her, her last thought was that she should have told him she loved him when she still had the chance.

Maybe in the next lifetime she'd get another shot at it.

14

It wasn't ending this way. He wouldn't let it.

Cris skidded to a halt on the far side of the barrier and then turned and charged back toward it.

The wall held, the water surging up against it without passing through. That was part of its design. It would allow slow-moving, solid objects to pass through, but atmosphere and, in this case, water, were held back. If Aria had been caught up in the wave, she might have washed up against the barrier or close to it.

He paced the length of the barrier, but he wasn't able to see much with the lights still off.

When they came back on again, they dazzled his eyes and left him blinking away the spots filling his vision. Once he could see again, he did another scan of the barrier. Where was she? Why hadn't she jumped clear or sprinted through the barrier before the water hit?

The answer hit him like a comet strike. The blaster. The scanners in this area would pick it up immediately, and now she no longer had the protection of a guest wristband... the station's automated defenses would have killed her the moment the weapon was detected.

The wall of water reminded him of the aquarium they'd visited earlier that day, and the primal part of his mind populated the newly formed sea with every dangerous marine creature they'd seen. He knew it was impossible, but that awareness wasn't enough to stop another surge of adrenaline from getting dumped into his system.

He'd have given anything to have Aria's implant right then. His average human eyes couldn't see far into the water, and the air wall created a blurring effect that made it even more difficult.

He forced himself to stay still, turning his head so that his peripheral vision came into play.

There!

Something moved at the corner of his eye and he turned to focus on it. There was a shadowy shape in the water to his right. Arms. Legs... *Fraxx.*

Aria was in trouble.

He toed off his boots with frantic speed, took a deep breath and then exhaled it all. Only then did he take one last breath to fill his lungs before pushing through the barrier.

Stepping into deep water was an odd sensation, but at least the water wasn't too cold. It stung the burned skin of his arm and sent ripples of pain through him, reminding him of the damage VIDA had inflicted during their brief connection.

He'd deal with that problem later. For now, he had to get to Aria. With that thought forefront in his mind, he pushed off the floor and started swimming.

She was barely moving, and most of her body was beneath the water. Her natural buoyancy and the design of her body armor should have brought her to the surface, but the strap of her bag had tangled around one foot and was weighing her down. If the water had been any deeper, she'd have drowned. Only her long legs and the length of the strap had allowed her head to break the surface.

He rose up beside her, careful not to make contact until his head was out of the water and she could see his face.

"Blink?" Her name came out in a rasp.

She moaned and turned toward him, revealing a nasty gash that ran from her eyebrow to her hairline and beyond.

"I got you, Ri. I just need to go down and untangle your foot, okay?"

Another groggy moan, though this time her eye lids fluttered open. "Mmhmm. Ow."

"Big ow. I thought we agreed there would be no drowning on a space station. Insubordination will not be tolerated. We'll discuss your punishment later."

Her eyes opened and she fixed him with a bemused if somewhat unsteady stare. "Punishment?"

"You disobeyed orders, Lieutenant."

"I'm going back to sleep now. When I wake up again, you better have forgotten this conversation ever happened."

He got them both back through the barrier without too much trouble. Aria didn't slip back into unconsciousness, but she stayed quiet and calm until they were back on dry footing.

Despite Cris's earlier instructions to get to the ship, Ramon hadn't left. He stayed to help, a fact Crispin was grateful for as they made their way to the ship as fast as they could. He had Aria in his arms, but Ramon fell in behind him, watching their backs and ensuring none of the beings in this part of the station came too close.

Soaking wet, shoeless, and panting with a semi-conscious woman in his arms, his wild appearance probably did as much to keep everyone away as the liaison's looming presence. Synda stood at the door, gesturing them in with sharp, worried motions as she scanned the corridor as though she expected all hell to break loose at any minute.

That's when he realized it had gone quiet. There

were no more power surges, and the grav-plates were no longer malfunctioning. No mad cackles or furious screams tore the air, and while the few souls he saw were wary and scared, they weren't panicking.

Synda withdrew into the *Vixen* as they approached, leaving the hatchway clear. Cris went first, shouting commands to the ship's AI the moment he was on board.

Then the lights came on in the docking area, and an alarm sounded while Ramon was still outside.

The station was coming back online. It was time to go.

He put Aria down in the corridor and Synda hurried over to help her. Cris gave her a grateful nod and then turned back toward the door, still issuing orders to the *Vixen's* AI. The moment that door closed, they needed to be gone.

Ramon should have been inside by then. He wasn't.

Cris dashed back to the door to find Ramon collapsed just a step away. He'd taken a blaster bolt to the shoulder and was barely conscious. Large security guards in Babylon's standard uniform raced down the corridor toward them.

He dug deep and found the strength to pull the big man inside the ship. As he wrestled him inside, Cris heard the same warning repeat several times. "Unauthorized staff departure. Stop where you are, or you will be shot."

They'd shot Ramon rather than allow him to leave. Even with everything else they'd handled, that fact hit harder than a rogue comet. If they ever came back here, it better be to take this place down forever.

He hauled Ramon far enough inside to get his feet clear of the door. The second the hatch sealed he called out, "Vixen, departure override activated. Punch it!"

Then he slid down to the floor, cradled a still-groggy Aria in his lap and leaned back against the bulkhead while Synda did the same for Ramon.

There was a scream of metal, several explosive thumps, and then they were free of their docking clamps and on their way.

Looking down at Aria, he found her smiling up at him, her hair plastered to her skin and blood smeared across one cheek.

They'd made it.

"Caldwell, if you don't let me off this *fraxxing* med-bed you will be the one who needs medical treatment," Aria grumbled. Cris had insisted she take the med while he got Ramon into the ship's onboard medical system, also known as a doc-in-a-box.

Synda sat beside the monitors, watching her life partner sleeping, but she tore her eyes away to smile at Aria. "You might want to cut him a little slack. He did save your life back there."

"He did." Aria caught Cris's hand to make him stop whatever scan he was running to look at her. "And if he'd hold still for more than two seconds, I'd like to say thank you."

He stilled. "You never have to thank me for that, Ri. If I'd lost you..."

The look he gave her was haunted by the shadows of what might have been. It tore at her heart and reminded her that there were things they still needed to say to each other—important things that would change the trajectory of their lives. The thought had terrified her until recently. Now the only thing that scared her was the thought she had almost missed out on a lifetime with Cris.

"The only way that's going to happen is if you don't let me up. All the scans were clear. I'm almost fully healed already, and you're just keeping me here because..." She narrowed her eyes at him.

He smirked.

"You son of a starbeast," she growled. "Is this my punishment?"

"Part of it," he admitted and powered down the energy field restraining her.

She was off the bed in seconds, using all her weight and enhanced strength to hit Cris with enough force to knock him off balance. She kept pushing until he leaned up against a bulkhead and then rose on her toes to kiss him. "Asshole."

He wrapped one arm around her waist and cradled the back of her head with the other. "I love you, too."

Need thrummed through her veins like liquid fire accompanied by feelings she'd denied for far too long. Love and desire surged to the forefront of her mind and her heart, but there was something new, too—a sense of belonging and perfect rightness that made her soul sing.

She fell into their next kiss hungrily. Tasting, touching... devouring every part of him. It wasn't until Synda made a soft noise somewhere between a laugh and a moan that she remembered they weren't alone.

"Sorry," Synda said. "Empath, remember? You two need to have some time alone. I'll stay with Ramon."

Aria nodded and deliberately focused her emotions, sending the other female a pulse of gratitude and reassurance. "We're safe now."

Synda nodded. "I believe you. But now we're free of that place, can you tell me who you really are?"

Cris chuckled. "I'm Lieutenant Crispin Caldwell, and this is Lieutenant Aria Jessop. We're with Nova Force."

Synda's silver eyes went impossibly wide. "Nova Force? Out here?"

Aria waved her hand in a vague, negating gesture and then winked. "We were never here, which is convenient for you because it means there will be no record of the two of you being delivered to one of the best-defended colonies in the known galaxy."

"Where is that? You mentioned Haven, but I haven't heard of it."

"You're going to the planet Liberty."

Synda's lower lip vanished between her teeth for a moment. "The Vardarian colony? Will they want us?"

"They will. And you'll be safe there. With fresh air, free water, and an entire world for your child to play in."

Synda wiped her hand across her eyes, but not before Aria saw the tears shimmering there.

"Thank you. You have no idea what this...I..."

Cris smiled the deep, satisfied smile of a man who had been given a gift without price. "You are so welcome."

Through their internal link, Aria asked another question. *"Is VIDA gone?"*

"I monitored the station's systems until we were out of range. No sign of either of them. It worked. In fact, it worked better than expected. The damage they did to Babylon's systems was enough to prevent the station from mounting any kind of attack on us as we left. Not a single shot fired and no sign of pursuit."

"Then you and I have a few things to say to each other in private." She paused before asking the one question she never expected to say to Crispin ever again. *"Your room or mine?"*

Her room was closer.

The moment they tumbled through the door his hands were everywhere, caressing her, holding her, undressing her with a hurried tenderness that melted her heart and made her ache with need and unfamiliar emotions.

Cris pressed her up against one wall, his body caging hers as he took what he needed from her lips, leaving her dizzy with desire.

"Say it," he whispered between torrid kisses. "I need to hear it, Ri."

She'd thought it would be hard to say. It wasn't. "I love you. I want to spend the rest of our lives driving each other crazy. I mean, I do if you do."

He caught her chin in his hand and locked eyes with her. "I have wanted that since the day we met. I will never *not* want to be with you. I love you, Aria Jessop."

Words failed her. Instead of speaking, she threw her arms around his neck and kissed him. It was hard and heated, teeth clicking, lips bruised, tongues tangled. He groaned, the sound little more than a deep rumble that rolled through her like thunder. It was music to hear ears, a promise of carnal delights to come.

This was what had been missing all this time—the part of her she'd been denying existed. A state of being that could only be attained when she finally admitted the truth. She'd been wrong. Cris made her a better person. A better soldier. He was the other half of her soul, and she never wanted to lose this feeling again.

Somehow they made it to the bed, mouths still locked together, hands flying and fingers fumbling as they undid each other's clothes. He pulled her into his arms, the warmth and strength of his body wrapping around hers as he tumbled them both backward onto the pile of pillows at one end of the bed.

She landed with her head on his bare chest, one of his arms folded across her shoulders and their legs tangled together. Her entire existence shrank down to just the two of them. Hard muscle and soft kisses. Caresses that left trails of fire in their wake and kindled searing flames of desire that burned with white hot intensity.

She touched him everywhere she could reach, learning every line and sinew of his body. The only part she avoided was the dressing on his arm. The burns were healing quickly, but the last thing she wanted to do was bring him any pain. This moment was all about pleasure.

They'd both risked their lives today and lived to tell the tale. Their jobs were dangerous, and there was no telling what or when their last mission might be. They might vanish like her parents or sail off into the stars in search of new adventures like Colonel Archer had done. She couldn't control or predict the future, but she could make sure that every day they were together, she and Cris would celebrate the time they had and whatever time they had left.

"Stop thinking," he ordered her between kisses. "We'll have time for that later."

She nipped his lip sharply. "The mission's over, which means you are not in charge of me anymore."

He reared back and fixed her with a stern stare that turned her brain to jelly and filled her stomach with mutant butterflies.

"The hell I'm not. I am personally taking charge of your body for the rest of your life. Every breath. Every moan. Every bit of your pleasure is mine, Aria Jessop. Forever." His words were low and deep, rolling through her like the slow chiming of a bell that resonated deep in her soul.

Her answer came as he skimmed a hand down her belly and plunged two fingers into the folds of her pussy. "Forever."

The moment the word sunset past her lips she knew it was true. It wasn't romantic or even well-timed, but it was the greatest truth of her life. She was his now... and always would be.

The air between them almost sizzled with the heat that blazed between them, and when his lips curved up into a sinful smile, she knew she was in the best kind of trouble.

His mouth wandered from her lips to her ear and then down the side of her throat. When he settled a knee between her spread thighs, she shimmied lower on the bed. She didn't stop until her core was pressed against the bare skin of his knee. She ground her clit against him, using him to get herself off as he kissed his way down her body. Sharp nips of his teeth and the soft caresses of his lips on her breasts and nipples took her closer to the release she craved.

She couldn't hold back her soft moans of need, but the moment she uttered a sound Crispin stopped what he was doing and raised his head.

"You've forgotten. Haven't you?" he asked.

"Forgotten what?" she was drunk with desire and her words came out breathy and soft.

"Part two of your punishment."

"Now?" Her eyes snapped open and she glared at him in disbelief and some amusement. "You're going to try and punish me now?" She sat up, deliberately arching her back to put her breasts on full display. "Are you sure that's what you want to be doing?"

"No. Yes. Wait. What was the question again?" Cris's gaze was nowhere near her eyes, and he was drinking in the sight of her naked body with obvious hunger.

She parted legs wider and lay back on the bed,

lifting her hips in a blatant invitation.

"Not a question. More like a choice. Punishment. Yes or no."

He licked his lips and pretended to consider his options. "You did break our agreement. No drowning on a space station."

"I did not drown, thank you very much. I was resting my eyes while taking an unexpected but delightfully refreshing swim."

He huffed with laughter. "So, no punishment needed?"

"None."

"And instead..." he prowled over to her, eyes hungry, muscles flexing beneath golden skin.

"You. Me. This." She crooked her finger at him. "Now."

"Yes, ma'am."

His tone made her shiver, every part of her aching for something only he could give her. That's when he finally moved, settling himself between her thighs. He dove in like a man starved, hands parting her folds, his tongue curling around her clit. Pleasure sizzled through her veins and flooded her senses as she lifted her hips to grind herself against his mouth.

His wicked tongue lashed at her clit, pushing her to her breaking point with a single-minded purpose that left her panting and wild. He kept her teetering on the edge of release without letting her go over, and just when she was ready to beg him to let her come, he drew the tender bundle of nerves deep into the heat of his mouth.

She came apart within seconds, her cries muffled by the velvet fabric covering the walls of her quarters. Cris didn't stop, though. He pushed her higher than she'd ever gone before, his tongue flicking across her clit with merciless speed. He left her limp and panting, her legs trembling as he gently pulled away.

Reality intruded slowly, bringing with it another rush of desire for the man who held her heart. "I love you," she whispered as she drew him close and kissed him, her fingers framing his face, the taste of her essence on his lips.

"And I love you. I think I have since the first time we did this." He moved over her, the heavy shaft of his cock sliding between her still-slick thighs to nestle against her entrance.

His mouth crashed down on hers as he claimed her, the two of them coming together in a storm of passion that stole her mind and left her riding a wave of pure pleasure. Words failed them both, but they didn't need them. Not anymore.

Limbs tangled as he drove her deeper into the mattress, each thrust and rise of their hips forming a dance of seduction as old as the stars outside. His cock filled her so tightly that every movement sent ripples of desire radiating through her. He varied the tempo, slow and deep, then hard and fast, every downward stroke sliding over her clitoris.

"Ri," he murmured her name between kisses, his tongue tracing her lips before slipping inside to tangle with hers. He fucked her with his cock and tongue, the two of them moving in synch as the rhythm of their lovemaking increased, hurtling them toward climax.

"I'm sorry," she whispered the next time she had breath to speak. She felt almost lost in that moment with regret for all the time she'd wasted.

"Never be sorry. Just be mine." Then he groaned and his control snapped, his expression shifting to one of pure rapture as they came together in perfect harmony. She orgasmed hard, her inner walls gripping his length so tightly she could feel his cock thicken and jerk as he came.

They stayed that way for a long time, tangled up and enjoying each other while they could. Moments like this were precious. And she wanted to steal as many of them as she could and gather them up for those times when they'd have to be apart. Not that she intended for there to be many such times. They'd fought side by side for years now. That wasn't going to change.

Whoever came for them next, whatever threats arose, they'd face it all together. The battle to safeguard the galaxy would continue... and so would the two of them.

EPILOGUE

Sitting in the rustic but comfortable setting of the Bar None Tavern with a full belly and a warmth that had more to do with the company than the temperature, Crispin finally understood why Aria had been so eager to return to Haven. Something about the colony called to him.

It wasn't the planet. Liberty was no better or worse than any other of the hundred worlds he had visited in his life. It was the beings who called this place home. They came from different species and different walks of life, but somehow they had formed a community with roots as deep as the mountains that lined the horizon. He'd only been on the planet once before, yet it already felt more like home than anyplace he'd been since he left his home world.

Or maybe, it was because Aria was here—not just on the same planet or at the same table, but in his life. Their hands were loosely clasped beneath the table even now, their chairs only a few inches apart. When she shifted in her chair, her shoulder would brush against his. Better yet, it took only a slight movement to press their thighs together beneath the table any time he wanted to. He did it a lot.

All around them people were laughing, joking, eating, and drinking. The tavern was filled with beings going about their lives. Most of them didn't even know why his team and their friends were celebrating, but the sense of levity and relief that accompanied them had been infectious and had spread everywhere.

Nico was gleefully making the rounds of the tables, sneaking tidbits from everyone he knew, which appeared to be nearly everyone present. They all pretended not to notice as he filched bits of food and popped them into his pockets or, more often, straight into his mouth.

It was one more thing Crispin liked about this place. They had clearly accepted Nico, a street urchin who had survived by himself on the streets of a rough and tumble world, without trying to change him. They simply accepted who he was and allowed him to carry on. It was why Crispin knew Synda and Ramon would do well here. In fact, he expected them to thrive.

Haven was a place of acceptance as well as a

place of safety. The young couple so recently freed from the bonds of servitude deserved both. Knowing that he and Aria had helped to make that happen was almost the best part of this day. But only almost. After all, today had also been Dante's wedding day. The small ceremony was attended by just the team and a few friends and hosted in the courtyard garden of the prince's home. Fresh snow had turned it into a wonderland, the bright light of the sun only dimmed when compared to the radiant beauty of the bride.

He'd stood witness as his friends spoke their vows, his fingers tangled with Aria's as they watched and then cheered when it was done.

Dante and Tyra were spending their wedding night alone while their adopted son was left in the care of the team for the evening. Magi had the current shift, and Aria and Cris had agreed to put the boy to bed on the *Malora* when the evening ended.

He hadn't been sure how Nico would react to the idea of he and Aria being together, but the boy had accepted it without question or comment... which was more than he could say about the rest of the crew. They hadn't questioned it either, but they'd made comments by the dozen. Most of them including the phrase "about *fraxxing* time."

Assholes, all of them. Assholes... and the best family a man could hope to find.

This party was as much for them as for any other

reason. The wedding celebration had ended hours ago, leaving the newlyweds alone to enjoy themselves while the party moved on to the Bar None. It was the same place they'd been to the last time they were here, a surprisingly good tavern in this newly built place, run by a tough-as-nails human female and her two very large Vardarian husbands.

With the team together again, and even Kurt's lover, Bobbi, in attendance for the wedding, their table at the tavern was as full as his heart. As he looked around the table, he realized this was the end of one chapter and the beginning of another. Somehow they had all found the other half of their heart and they'd all fight like hell to protect the ones they loved from any threat.

And there were more than enough threats out there. Even with the death of Absalom and the elimination of VIDA, the Grey Men were still out there, diminished but still dangerous. There would always be corporations to hold in check and innocent beings to protect from predators.

He squeezed Aria's hand under the table, his thigh touching hers. She leaned in and kissed him, and somehow he knew she was thinking the same thing he was. The fight wasn't over, and it wouldn't be for a long, long time. It didn't matter, though, because no matter what might come for them, Aria would always have his back... and his heart.

Forever.

***

Thank You for Reading Operation Sunset!

If you want to know more about this world and the Colony of Haven, I invite you to explore the other books in the rest of Drift universe - including the Nova Force, The Drift, and **Haven Colony** series. Keep reading for a look at Her Alien Mates, first book in the Haven Colony series.

Shadow put away her hand terminal and stylus and then got to her feet, her head full of new data and fascinating tidbits. Her onboard systems had the entire lecture itemized and stored for future reference, but she'd discovered that the act of writing notes helped her think about them as more than abstract facts. It was one of the many things she'd learned about herself since arriving at Haven.

"Hey, Shadow, joining us for drinks?" Skye asked. The cyborg female was part of the panel that had presented today's session on sexuality, mating, and courtship rituals.

"Sure." She grinned at her mentor. "Do I get to ask more questions?"

Skye laughed. "Only if you're buying."

"Deal." She had more than enough scrip to her name to afford a few drinks. She'd been offered the same corporate-sponsored compensation package as the other cyborgs living here. They had all been held captive, some of them for years, and the corporations had turned a blind eye to their existence. As far as Shadow was concerned, giving them a bit of money and a place to live was the least the bastards could do.

She walked with the others, letting the conversation flow around her without taking an active part. Shadow hadn't been held captive with Skye and the rest of the cyborgs at the colony. Her experience had been very different. She'd been kept isolated from almost everyone for most of her life, and as much as she enjoyed the comradery, it took some getting used to.

Her freedom had come only recently, and she was still adjusting to a reality where she could make all her own choices. There were no punishments, no threats, and no one issuing orders she had no choice but to obey. Just thinking about it triggered a rush of unwanted memories. Recollections of all the things she'd done against her will pushed in on her until it was hard to breathe.

She slowed her steps and looked up into the wide blue sky. "I'm free," she reminded herself softly. A glint of gold caught her attention, and she turned her gaze to the high-flying form of a Vardarian wheeling through the endless blue. She envied them their wings. If she could fly like they could, she'd never want to land.

"You okay?" Skye asked.

"Memory ambush," Shadow explained. The first thing she'd learned at the colony was to be honest about how she felt. It wasn't always easy, but after a lifetime of hiding their thoughts and reactions, it was freeing to be able to talk about it all.

"Ugh, I hate those. You okay now? Or do you want to take some time on your own?" Skye asked.

"I think I'm good. Besides, I still have questions!"

"Drinks first." Skye slid a companionable arm around her shoulders. "And nice job fending off the ambush. It took me months before I could move past them as fast as you can. Care to share the trick?"

Shadow pointed up. "It's easy to remember I'm free when there's nothing above me but open sky."

"Which is exactly why I picked my name." The cyborg turned her head to glance at her. "Can I ask why you picked Shadow?"

"Because I was cloned from a cyborg who called herself Nyx. Apparently, that was the name of an old Earth goddess of night who was also the daughter of chaos. I'm sort of her daughter...so I figured, Shadow."

"I like it. Even though you are the least dark and shadowy person I have ever met."

Shadow appreciated the compliment, but she knew it wasn't true. She'd been created as part of the

Fury project, and while there had been some minor adjustments to their design, all the furies had one thing in common. They were assassins.

Most corporate-created cyborgs were soldiers. A handful were made to serve other purposes. Some were spies. Others were capable of incredible data processing that made them almost prescient. She and her sisters—the furies—were executioners.

"C'mon. It's time for drinking, not thinking," Skye teased and pointed ahead of them. "After all that talk about sexuality, pleasure, and mating, the males of this place better watch out. I'm thinking about taking a few of them home with me tonight!"

"A few?" Shadow was intrigued by the idea of having more than one mate, but her seduction programming had all involved enticing one being at a time. And her personal experiences... well, she might have been ordered to sleep with various beings, but she'd never made that choice for herself.

"Why not? That's how most Vardarian relationships are structured, and the ratio of male to female cyborgs skews heavily to the males." Skye shrugged. "And for me, it's all about blowing off steam. I'm not looking for a relationship. I just want to have fun."

Shadow nodded, but she felt a discordant twinge of emotional energy from her companion that told her Skye wasn't being entirely honest. She did want more, but she couldn't admit it yet. Fair enough.

They were all on a journey, and it wasn't her place to try to change someone else's trajectory just because she could tell what they were feeling.

"What about you? You ready to find a little fun? Or maybe put some of the things you learned today into practice?" Skye waited a beat before casually adding, "Like, oh, flirting with a certain broody Torski male who happens to be due back this afternoon?"

"Denz is home?" Her query somehow bypassed all her internal filters and was out of her mouth before she could zip her lips shut.

Skye's blue eyes flashed in triumph. "Ha! I knew it."

"Does everyone know?" One thing Shadow had learned in her time here was the colony's cyborgs were the biggest gossips in the galaxy. They shared data files and tidbits of information with breathtaking speed and unrepentant glee, and she had a great many reasons to keep her interest quiet.

"I don't think so. I'm training to be a counselor, and I'm your mentor. It's my job to watch out for you and make sure you're acclimating to your new life. That means I'm paying more attention than most. I saw your face when you heard he was leaving." Skye winked. "And I'd bet another round of drinks that at least one of the questions you wanted to ask me about had to do with Torski courtships."

"Anyone ever mention that you'd have made an excellent spy?" she asked.

"Me? *Fraxx*, no. I think it's more that you're becoming a worse one. When you first got here you had three expressions, and only one of them involved smiling. Now, you're not hiding your feelings as much. It means you're settling in."

Shadow twisted a lock of hair around her finger and tugged. "I guess. But that's really not information I'm ready to share. I mean, I like him, but trying to initiate anything with Denz would be...complicated."

"Maybe." Skye pitched her voice low enough so there was no chance of being overheard. "But you're not the one who pulled the trigger. He knows that."

Shadow tugged a little harder on her hair. "I might not be the one who murdered Zale, but you can't tell by looking at me. The killer was my clone. Same face. Same design. Same programming."

Skye grunted. "What was the first thing I told you when you and I started talking?" She asked as they crossed the bridge to the small island that sat midway between the cyborg and Vardarian sides of the colony.

"We're more than our programming," Shadow answered automatically.

"Exactly. And Denz has been around cyborgs enough to know that too."

He'd said as much to her the first time they'd

met, but she'd sensed the unease he felt being around her. Hell, she hadn't needed to be empathic to tell he avoided being in her company for long. Once she'd gotten more settled and started exploring, they'd crossed paths more and more often. Every time it happened he'd made himself scarce within minutes. Then, he'd volunteered to leave the colony on a diplomatic mission that had kept him away for weeks. She might not have a lot of experience discerning other beings' personal motivations, but his had been as clear as the air above her. Denz Talorn didn't want to be on the same planet as her.

She shrugged. "I know he doesn't blame me. But not holding me accountable for Zale's death is a few hundred light-years away from wanting to share a meal or a drink...or any of the other dating rituals I've been learning about. I have no idea how to get him to think of me that way."

Skye's peals of laughter carried across the water and blended with the burble of the river as it flowed beneath them. "I am about to tell you one of the secrets of the universe—a truth that was taught to me by the princess herself." She leaned in and whispered in Shadow's ear. "Males are not complicated. If you like him, tell him so."

"Nothing in life is that easy. What if he doesn't like me?"

Skye shrugged. "Then he'll say so. It'll sting for a few minutes. Phaedra also taught me that copious amounts of ice cream can be used to moderate emotional pain. She recommended chocolate."

"I don't think I'm ready for that, but...I'll remember about the ice cream. Just in case."

They reached the front doors of the Bar None and she followed Skye inside. This would be so much easier if she were Vardarian. They didn't fall in love the way humans did. They scented their mates and were overtaken by the *sharhal*, the mating fever. It wasn't emotionally driven at all. It was a biological response, pure and simple.

She thought about that for a moment and then decided she didn't want that either. She'd lived most of her life without the freedom to choose for herself. Given the choice between random biology and risking rejection... *fraxx* it. Maybe she'd just stay single.

*

Ready for more? Pick up Her Alien Mates and keep reading.

ABOUT THE AUTHOR

Susan lives out on the Canadian west coast surrounded by open water, dear family, and good friends. She's jumped out of perfectly good airplanes on purpose and accidentally swum with sharks on the Great Barrier Reef.

If the world ends, she plans to survive as the spunky, comedic sidekick to the heroes of the new world, because she's too damned short and out of shape to make it on her own for long.

To contact her about her books or to arrange end of the world team-ups, you can email her at susan@susanhayes.ca.

For all titles by Susan Hayes, please visit her website:
susanhayes.ca